It's Over

Lee K. Sanford

Order this book online at www.trafford.com
or email orders@trafford.com

Most Trafford titles are also available at major online book retailers.

Printed in Victoria, BC, Canada.

ISBN: 978-1-4269-2738-6 (sc)

*We at Trafford believe that it is the responsibility of us all, as both individuals
and corporations, to make choices that are environmentally and socially sound.
You, in turn, are supporting this responsible conduct each time you purchase a
Trafford book, or make use of our publishing services. To find out how you are
helping, please visit www.trafford.com/responsiblepublishing.html*

*Our mission is to efficiently provide the world's finest, most comprehensive
book publishing service, enabling every author to experience success.
To find out how to publish your book, your way, and have it available
worldwide, visit us online at www.trafford.com*

Trafford rev. 02/19/2010

 www.trafford.com

North America & international
toll-free: 1 888 232 4444 (USA & Canada)
phone: 250 383 6864 ✦ fax: 812 355 4082 ✦ email: info@trafford.com

This book is dedicated to those Americans whose American dream has been turned into the American nightmare.

CHAPTER 1

Another day in this filth ridden apartment on Milwaukee's north side, and as I wake I am accompanied by the familiar feeling of a great hangover. My eyes are stuck together with a glue like substance, my throat is as dry as sandpaper, and my right shoulder is in some serious agony. I love the half inflated air mattress I awake upon and realize I have been sleeping on my right should over a nice cold hard wood floor. As I muster the energy to roll off the mattress and unto the floor I smell the fragrance of a hard night, rather hard living lifestyle with not much to offer. I am sure many of you reading this know what I am talking about. That stale smell of cigarette smoke and beer mixed along with the scent of ones own urine and body odor. Yes isn't life just grand! I gain my footing and am shocked at the damage done to not only myself but the entire apartment. Beer cans litter the ground like grass, cigarette butts in bowls of half eaten pasta, just a nice array of total annihilation. I need some serious water as my throat is like a dry desert and my head begins to let me know of the circulation process.

The apartment I should also describe probably in a little detail before I go further to paint a better image to you. It is a kitchen on the right side of the domicile and my bedroom and living room on the left with a shared bathroom in the hallway with another housemate. The floors are all hardwood with a nice high ceiling

I believe it is in the style of some Victorian but I am uncertain. In the kitchen there is a full fridge and stove both of which often are not working or I have to go and jiggle the plug-ins risking electrocution to see if I can get them to work. The sink is one of those old school cast iron outfits I believe very old and very used, along with some rickety cabinets.

The kitchen is where I believe a lot of the roaches seem to make their mass entrance into my place. I also often find them in my bedroom portion of the place and try to extinguish their lives as quickly as possible but realize damn they are quick. The place is quite a dump nothing seems to work all the time at the same time and the noise in the neighborhood, whether it is crack heads or sirens or the occasional gun shot would make any place a total dive. Now that the setting in which this initial orientation has been somewhat described I will get back to my pounding unbelievable headache and other morning tasks.

Like I said my head was pounding quite a bit and the urge for water was comparable to the urge of having some good sex. I gain access to the faucet and turn the knob with great difficulty as my hands are somewhat shaky and my eyes are still stuck half shut with gunk I try to navigate this great task. The splash of the water down onto the sink coming out with the force of a hose spraying down blacks in the civil rights movement, I put my mouth to the water and spray half of it on myself as well as down my throat: what a relief hydration at last! As I whip my head back and put my hands under the hurricane of water coming out I wipe the gunk out of my eyes as to regain my proper vision.

After I accomplished these little tasks I look into the mirror in my bedroom it is one of those duel usage items a dresser with a mirror on top I believe they are also cited as Dutch dressers? I realize I have been wearing some pretty dirty and quite smelling clothes. The gray sweatpants that I enjoy and the white wife beater that has now become a mixed color something that Pollock might have painted. And to be honest I could care less as to what

I look like or to some extent how I feel I only see total and utter defeat and rage in that mirrored picture of myself.

As I stand there staring somewhat like a zombie at my own reflection I grasp the sound of Marvin Gays what's going on in my housemate's room across the hall. Now my housemate is quite a character my goodness a total drunk to the fullest. I don't really mind Motown music I am rather fond of it but this gentleman plays it like we are in some concert hall and with this hangover it is not sounding to pleasant. What am I supposed to do I have only met the man a few times and usually brief passes hello, goodbye, what's up things of that nature. Now being a white male in an all black neighborhood I didn't want to ruffle anybody's feathers because I didn't want to get into any trouble. Yes the stereotyping of blacks being quick to violence and rage was in my head at the time I confess.

Well I decided that I needed to grab another cold one more urgently than trying to tell my neighbor housemate to turn the music down. Oh yes let me tell you about the contents in my full size frigerator. I am sure there are some bachelors reading this so I am sure you all will take great joy in this itemized declaration. Oh lets see usually the fridge is full of beers however the previous evening, rather whole day I seemed to consume most of them so there was only three sixteen ounce beers left. The rancid bologna meat in the far right side with that nice green like grass growing plentiful upon it. The apple sauce for some reason I purchased because I was going to buy steaks and eat it with that but that didn't happen. Ranch dressing yes indeed need that for ahhhhm you know chicken wings, and anything else your heart desires when you get fully intoxicated, but the ranch looked and smelled a bit funky. Grape jelly of course for those peanut butter and jelly sandwiches who can deny their useful stomach stuffing importance when you are on a seven dollar budget for four days. Unfortunately I seem to be all out of peanut butter how surprising. Eggs, let us not forget eggs, you can make egg salad, scrambled eggs, and regular eggs these I have found to be of great use to a

3

poor bastard like myself and I find they unlike peanut butter and jelly are often used with great urgency and timeliness.

Enough as I am sure you are thinking about this boring discussion of my refrigerators contents. Anyway off I go into the world this day I need some food and need to check for job postings in this great economy. I drive a dependable Saturn two door coupe it's a 98 and has plenty of miles on it but hey beats the bus. The key in the ignition and the ding of my light on the dashboard like a damn hammer and anvil sound makes me aware of the fact that I am on fumes. So I am off to the gas station and as I pull in I open my wallet to find approximately eighty cents, and I look into my center board and see, oh my goodness, another fifty cents! So I have a whopping dollar thirty to purchase gas with my goodness. As I enter the gas station there is a line and my anxiety and embarrassment mounts as I throw my change under the fortress of a piece of glass and tell the attendant, "one thirty on pump four". The man is of some near Asian decent and with a strong accent and look of disbelief says, "Soddy one dolla tirdy cent?" I go yes please and as I leave I feel filled with rage as I am embarrassed but also angry at the fact that this gentleman I know owns this station and is clearly a new comer to this country. I say to myself how can they do it? Own there own establishment and barely speak English and here I am a college graduate and I cannot even get a ten dollar an hour job: my discontentment overflows.

I pull away with the gas showing just at the empty level not on fumes but will be shortly. I cannot help but scream and say what the fuck is happening here? I drive to the library to engage in job hunting and think what kind of opportunities are here for the American? The guy or gal who has done for the most part the right things. What is this going to be a fricken third world existence in a first world country? I am not sure all I realize is that shit isn't working out for me here in Milwaukee. I came here about 7 seven months ago from Ann Arbor Michigan that topic we'll delve into at a later time.

Now I have to utilize the library because I do not have a Mac whatever with three billion gigs or megs or whatever the hell the terminology is of computers. Oh yes the library experience I am sure you the reader if ever unfortunate to have to use a library in an over crowded city with an under supply of computers can probably appreciate this. I enter and to no surprise all the damned computers are occupied. Now there is a one hour time limit but it's really not enforced so like a bum I wait my turn. I have no job, no lady friend, or anything to attend to so what the hell right I mean put on that happy let me take a number face like at the DMV office. What's that I think someone is leaving no damn they were just printing something off. I am bored so I go kind of peeking at what the hell these kids are doing on the computers that should make me wait. To add fuel to my fire I realize none of the people are searching for work on monster or career builder which I was going to do. No instead with the free computers available to them I see hip hop dot come, face book, MySpace oh Jesus. Now I am sure I am sounding a bit snobby even like an asshole, but I want to find work and rationalize to myself my rage is valid and that the library should put away some computers for actual job hunting or other more mind stimulating searches that what I just witnessed here.

Oh does it suck not being anybody and not having a way to change some things the feeling of total impotence washes over me. Finally the computer opens up my god I feel like a person at the doctor's office waiting to be called and once your name is you feel like you won a prize not realizing an hour of your life just was pissed down the preverbal drain. To make this quick no fricken good jobs were on the sites what a surprise the few that were there paid twenty thousand or less. Most were basically ten an hour or less, but like the good worker bee America has turned us into I applied for the few slave wage jobs and hope for them, yeah hope for a ten dollar an hour job that I cannot possibly even live on.

Screw this I am done heading back to my shit hole apartment living with the walking dead, and as I leave the library I get hit up for some change. Oh how I cannot even know how to describe how damn tired I am of being hit up no matter where I go for fitty cent, then I say no then they say twenty five cent, I say no man then the unrelenting son of a bitch will ask for a smoke I mean I think if I gave them a pair of my dirty underwear they would take that shit anything and for nothing I swear they would take it. This pan handling or as I call it extreme pan handling is of a much more aggressive nature. I mean I almost like the guy that is sitting in his soiled pants and a jar in front of him not saying anything. In fact I would welcome more of them and would gladly toss them a bit of change. Now the extreme panhandler is aggressive, and comes up to you un announced something that I take seriously because I like my eighteen inch me space and they do not adhere to that. I don't know this inner city experience along with this unemployment shit this damn country is really starting to make me feel like Michael Douglas in the movie falling down. The white guy that just keeps getting tested by everyone and no color or gender lets him slide assuming he's a pussy a push over that he has money shit like that. The kind of thinking a lot of people come to ascribe when thinking of the white American male today.

Well it is time to cool down a bit as I return to my humble abode. I cannot help but feel this sick almost rotting feeling brewing inside of my mind and soul. It is something to be honest I have never experienced before in all my life. Now granted I have had some difficult times and trials but this is different and very uncanny. I am trying to figure out what exactly it is, is it some mental condition or has somebody put a curse on me I am so very uncomfortably unsure. That night I am feeling it even worse and now I have been in Milwaukee for a few months now and unemployed for oh let's say seven, and I am in serious state of what the fuck. Basically its hopelessness I am feeling a sense of the good times has long passed and I merely exist in this dimension. I mean I think to myself I know I haven't been perfect and made some mistakes some of which were somewhat big. I know that alcohol hasn't positively contributed, but I still feel overall I've made for the most part good decisions.

I completed my four year bachelors at Central Michigan University which was difficult for me to do. You know everyone back in the late nineties was saying college, college, college it opens doors for you all that shit. Well my experience is that it also closes doors for you as well. You come out of college twenty five to thirty five thousand dollars in debt so you cannot simply work a job that pays garbage you have to make a certain amount of money in order to even pay interest on those damned things. I see people that work at gas stations or what have you, you know the kind of rough looking chain smoking persons who barely graduated high school and went to work right away. Shit those people are actually smart especially now in 2008 with this great economy. I feel sorry for the idealistic kids graduating from college now. If I could do it over I would of either majored in something like health care, criminal justice, or law not fricken business administration, and I probably would have taken my time and paid as I went while still working a full time job.

Getting to the good times have passed idea, I have a friend that worked for a major car company in Michigan for thirty years no college straight out of high school. It was a family affair his mother and sister both also worked at the plant. He made a great living had job security and benefits was able to buy and pay off his house in a timely manner always having a nice car. He eventually took a buyout and a nice pension and health care for life to retire at fifty four. Now this friend I have I love him do not get me wrong but that shit is long gone today. In fact back home I here all the jobs are being cut and I see on the news people panicking. They all should be lucky they had that gravy train for as long as they did because today's youths and young people cannot be an uneducated and a basic skilled worker making sixty to seventy thousand a year to put a bolt in a frame. Now there are some people that worked at those plants that were skilled in their trade and did I believe a pretty damn good salary just for the record. And to be honest some of the unions are to be blamed for their increased greed and lack of flexibility as well as the management and the CEO. Other top officer assholes getting ridiculous compensation packages too it is ridiculous: overall though I still side with the union worker over management.

I guess that's one of the ideas that's really bothering me this evening as I try to think of the horrible feeling of hopelessness that invades my thoughts. It's the total and absolute feeling that the good times are gone that I came into this society to late that there is nothing for my generation but low paying jobs a type of indentured servitude. I have applied and looked a lot since moving to Milwaukee and there isn't much. I think to myself will I be living in rooms at thirty fucking years old or for the rest of my life? Work demeaning jobs with no future or security, and being broke even a few days after paid day I mean its making me really want to give up.

Well it is Wednesday morning today and this is the big day I get to call Michigan's unemployment service and try to get through and register for my next two weeks of benefits. I simply hate this day, I mean I don't know how many people reading this have had to try to get through especially to Michigan's automated system, but believe me its very frustrating. I have to call between eleven a.m and noon eastern time so that means since I am in central time I set my alarm for ten a.m because lord knows I would not get up at that hour by myself. Now after you dial this eight hundred number it will usually ring once and then say, "all circuits are busy please try again", or "thank you for calling Michigan's automated telephone system you can call me Marvin". I mean when I hear that great distinguished voice of Marvin when I call it is like a old friend inviting me over for dinner, however usually after thirty minutes of calling repeatedly do you get him.

We are in business I got through in approximately twenty minutes today and qualified and my check will be deposited into my account in two days hooray! I am pretty pleased this morning as my account is negative a few hundred dollars mostly in over drawn fees from my Nazi bank and I have virtually no food in my fridge. I really have little patience for the customer service side of this, it is a totally different number and once you get through you get someone with the worst damn attitude possible. I swear these people should be thankful to have a state job with probably great benefits, but ohhh no god forbid you ask these assholes a few questions especially if you are the unfortunate soul who is calling regarding the fact that your payment was not deposited in its normal time. I am sure many of you will say that they are busy and have a huge work load all that garbage, please don't waste your breath on this person because after trying to get a choice job like that sitting on my ass and hearing the morons that I have encountered on there I just cannot empathize with that.

Since I know my employment is coming I settle down a bit and try to put on that happy face. So what the hell have a few beers and celebrate right? I also realize that I do not have enough beers to get my fill and proceed to venture over to the market and re stock my supply. I shop at a place in downtown Milwaukee it's pretty nice and I know the liquor cashier guy. I really think this man hates my guts as well because no matter how many times I try to make small talk you know be the friendly customer and all he just gives me a half ass grin and a look of fuck off get your shit and be gone. Now maybe this is my perception well it is actually but I think most people know when someone is basically uncomfortable with them or just hates there lives and lets you know that they also hate you. Nevertheless, the purchase must happen and Lee must get his fill like George Thorgood would say.

The typical purchase for me would be four sixteen once pack of cans of the best brew ever brewed, Milwaukee's best ice. No people I am just kidding, but hey it does the trick and considering each of them only cost $2.25 for four you can see that not only do I enjoy blowing me liver up, but I am also a bit of an economic man as well.

Upon my return to my place I am hit with this feeling of total déjà vu. I have done this countless times and am starting to think to myself the feeling of neglect. The fact that I am neglecting my health and also the fact of my endless feelings of being less than that have haunted me ever since I was a child. Now I am not saying my parents let me live in a box under the house and that I was not fed I mean emotionally I felt neglected and to some extent I now feel by drinking all the time I am somehow neglecting my own self. I want things to be perfect you know the car, kids, great job, and hot wife but that's just plain naïve. How immature does that sound or to some extent unrealistic and yet I cannot help but think because I do not have these certain aspects in my life that I am justified in this action of self neglect. Although how unrealistic is it these things for which I have just mentioned? Why is it unrealistic to have what I consider to be the typical American dream? As I mentioned a bit earlier the good times are over or if not over damned hard to come by. Anyway on with the guzzle I have plenty and some food in the fridge also now and after running those few errands I must hit the tube and see what I will watch until I pass out in roughly six hours.

The history channel could be a possibility as I notice they are running a mini-marathon on the seven deadly sins that could take up most the time, or maybe the discovery channel. But first I must down a few beers as I am not managing my person to well. There we go a nice flood of relief goes down the hatch and instantly I am ready to continue this hunt for entertainment. The discovery channel has this show called, "A Haunting", on where they do re-enactments of people who have claimed to be haunted I find this show very tempting as well. Besides that on the tube of which I have like a hundred channels I settle on the seven deadly sins programming on the history channel. The first one I see is based on envy and boy I might not be able to get through this because as I am sure many of you are thinking, "This guy is dripping wet with it!"

I have to say probably that I am in many of ways but I wouldn't say that I envy really any body specific more less the materials or women that I would like to have yet do not possess. You know being alone and having all this time to oneself gives you a great opportunity to look inside, and this programming is making me a bit uncomfortable. After a mere ten minutes of this show I shut it off and say fuck this show. Obtaining another beverage I light a smoke on my stove and take a hefty inhale and crack the beer. This is bullshit, total bullshit I say to myself. Fuck this envy shit I don't envy the male who takes his balls off once getting married, having to work like a dog to keep his fat wife happy with plenty of food and clothes.

The rage is eating me alive I swear it. I try to calm myself down thinking of something pleasant, but I cannot be in my Zen mind pond I am not the Zen master. Forget about it like I said before I was neglecting my feelings trying to wash it away with booze no I will allow myself to be a total sore and let the pain be recognized. Boy this could get terribly ugly I think to myself and notice I am shaking and at the verge of tears not because of the booze no but because I do not know what to do with these feelings that inhabit my soul or mind or whatever the fuck.

I start thinking to myself well many people find fulfillment in music, gardening, what have you, and then I say aloud who are you fucking kidding? Like those things mean a damn thing to me, "what actually does then?" pops into my head. What means something to me is all the shit that I totally despise, I am screwed royally and come to the surmise that I really have neglected myself spiritually, emotionally, and physically for a long time. I indeed have wallowed and barely lived and am now a total cripple of a human being. Realizing this I have to take a break I don't know if any of you reading this have come to this notion of yourself, but let me tell you once you do a big black pit is where you are standing with you at the bottom.

CHAPTER 2

I would like to transition a bit into my housemate I mentioned briefly earlier and describe some encounters and aspects of him to you all. Bobby is an African American man in his early fifties I believe he mentioned once to me. I met Bobby the first day I rolled into Milwaukee and Bobby was a short man barely over five feet six inches tall with a medium complexion and wore simple attire consisting of a flannel type long sleeved shirt, a cap, and some basic khaki pants. I met him in our shared area of the bathroom between both our rooms. I introduced myself and he likewise as we made a simple but pleasant first meeting. I noticed as he hobbled my way there was something wrong with his leg and he smelt of a thick odor of alcohol. I didn't inquire as to the cause of his limp as I could tell he probably had something else better brewing back in his room as well as the fact that I could tell he wasn't that impressed with myself either.

Overall after first meeting him I thought that indeed this man is going to be interesting to say the least and proceeded back to unloading my possessions. As stated in the first part of this story I briefly described the interior part of my apartment here in Milwaukee, now I would like to describe the actual neighborhood as well as Bobby.

The parking area I had was in the back with access from the alleyway a gravel type drive way. I had a decent back porch on the back with a white lawn chair that had a wire wrapped around it to a lock making it fixed to the railway of the porch. I found this terribly funny the fact that someone would think so highly of a plastic white lawn chair, but I also remember thinking to myself, "oh shit this could have been a really, really bad idea". Anyway the first few days and weeks I pretty much was keeping to myself taking in the new found surroundings that were totally foreign to me. I can remember thinking of how a single black person must feel when in a school or environment of all white people and how vulnerable they too must feel. It didn't take long before I had to get to know some people and bobby was first on my list.

Bobby enjoyed listening to r&b, and other rap music outside a lot while sipping the finest malt liquor around. So one day I went out to talk with bobby on the porch. It was a sunny day pretty hot towards the end of august and plenty of neighborhood entertainment to observe. Bobby's sound system was a beat up old school type boom box, the quality wasn't great, but I imagine once you're that inebriated everything sounds just right. "What's up playa", bobby sounds off to me, I say simply and a bit shocked "not much just was enjoying the music and weather". We kind of sat there looking out onto the nice view of north 6th street, and I think that's the first time I saw the total shithole of an area that I had parachuted myself into. Trash everywhere I mean everywhere, a house across the street with boarded up windows looked like it was fire bombed.

Little kids running around with no socks, shoes, or shirts on looking dirty as hell. I saw a girl riding her bike in front of the house when suddenly she came to a hard and complete tumble. I ran over to her to assist her and she shoved me away with a look of total resentment: I was shocked.

After a few tense minutes of that Bobby and I started talking, mostly him actually as my head was still spinning taking all this in. He started to let me know in a very obvious way that I wasn't a normal fixture around these parts and that I needed to behave and speak in certain ways, or rather when not to speak. He started by saying to trust no one that everyone is out to get you and everything that you possess and if you give them a chance they will rob you blind. I remember him saying that he never allows people in the front onto his porch because they will try to get his beer that they will want to use the bathroom as a guise of looking around his place to see what is of value that can be looted. Now I admit I am not street if you will type of a man and all this seemed to be very interesting but also very sad to me.

He went on in a drunken tirade basically letting me know if I didn't already know that I am white and that the people around here are going to test and try me to the best of their abilities. Well at first I didn't like the racial overtones that were being sad as well as for the implication that I as a white male am a pussy and a mark and that I could not defend myself if need be or acknowledge a seedy situation. Yeah like I said I knew that bobby was going to be an interesting character alright and I didn't know whether or not I wanted to know this man either after that.

With all that being said and with the fact of my emotions just barely kept under control I sought out the liquor store on the corner of 7th st. As I walked there I couldn't help bet again feel really naked totally being watched almost like hands being put all over me a total feeling of being molested. When I passed a few people I tried to instigate a friendly hello and I wasn't even acknowledged. My heart honestly was starting to produce a higher volume of blood into me and I started to think to myself what if I get mugged right now, and if I do shit its broad day light: a total mind fuck for me. The store was nothing to brag about a typical liquor store and the regulars that inhabit it I suppose. The bum outside asking for a few dimes, the barred up windows and the glass that covered the attendant in case of some robbery attempt.

Once in the store I felt a bit better and I made my selection and proceeded to move on and out the door. The walk back was interesting just as the walk there was a bit terrifying. I could here the rush of traffic passing on Locust Street and the interstate, the sound of music playing along with some women yelling at her kids. A nice pit-bull barking as if infected with rabies. Yeah I could tell this was going to be a great experience I just hoped I could get a job quickly and get the hell out of dodge.

When I approached the back to our place bobby was still there doing some kind of yell that let me know he was in good form. It was kind of like Rocky Balboa's scream to Adrian you know the "yooooo Adrian!", but it started with a yeah component then into yo something like yeaaaaoooohhhhhh! I could barely contain the laughter I mean I was ready to burst along with my sixteen ounce beer cans coming threw the plastic bags. The funny thing also was that no one around blinked or took notice of this and so I could only conclude that bobby is a fixture out here and that these antics are not unusual. I said to myself what the hell have a cold one or as bobby said, "hey man you gonna slam a few cold ones?" I figured absolutely I will slam a few I mean this is almost like the movies I thought to myself what characters and what drama lay just barely beneath. I couldn't also put my finger on the tunes he was playing it was obviously not my generations era and wasn't all that bad pretty laid back ballad type music. Well after a few cold ones as bobby would say I figured my little school trip was finished and sought refuge in my room.

The following day I have to start to try to get a job here and at first I am somewhat optimistic as the paper here seems to have some good leads as well as on the internet. I applied to three different staffing agencies here hoping that they could assist me a bit quicker in the hunt. I received a call from one of the ads I believed I applied to online and was set for a job interview or so I thought. I get all dressed up believing man this isn't going to take me that long to find employment here in Milwaukee and soon as I walk in I realize it was a staffing agency posing as an employer hiring. Now these types of techniques would become all too familiar I would find out later but I was a bit pissed off. I mean seriously I have no problem with meeting with a staffing agency, however I very much dislike having to get all dressed up in order to meet them under the pretense that this could be the actual interview that leads to a job not just the first part.

The guys I met also were a bunch of total douche bags. I mean the clean cut barely out of college white guys who were all like, "yeah man", or "great absolutely", and my personal favorite, "man we are the best in the business". What a mind fuck as I leave the office I see a bunch of people who probably already knew that this was a staffing agency and showed up in street clothes I was very angry.

Now a lot of this type of shit happens to me it seems a lot the false hope. Anyway I will not be discouraged right I will be the determined little worker bee I will work my ass off for shit pay and love it I will be quiet and not question work practices basically a total drone. The drive back to the hood was interesting I mean picture a white guy with a suit on driving around the walking deads houses and neighborhoods boy I felt like a target was right on the car. Well I guess I shouldn't worry about the walking dead zombies too much I mean for all intensive purposes I am one now too.

That was a nice sunny day though I can remember coming back from the jerk off meeting, very hot, low cloud cover and a perfect day to go do something. I probably back in Ann Arbor would have tried to go out with a friend or something, but here since I have no friends I started to realize how difficult this voyage would be for me psychologically. I mean I haven't made my loneliness a mystery so far I hope but it was going to be a difficult road to get on my feet and establish new contacts and peers since I was stashed away with the zombies.

With nothing else on the agenda this day I say what is in the fridge and what is on TV. Indeed this routine I have is very dull I mean I am starting to get totally comfortable like Pink Floyd says with being numb. The flow of booze starts the nasty clothes that haven't been washed in sometime and smell horrendous are put on the cigarette lit the programming being programmed ahh man this is the life.

Knock knock whose there I say and to my surprise the reply comes back with, "bobby man". This is a nice happening and I could use some company so I let him in and he's looking like his usual self the wool hat on even though its 80 out side, the flannel, and basic pants right on I say he wears the same shit often like me. "So what's happenin man", bobby says and I say, "Just slammin a few cold ones you know", using his distinct vernacular. I could tell he wanted one of those cold ones I was handling and as a matter of politeness I didn't want to not offer a guest for the first time into my place something so I grabbed him one and said here.

I figure this should be interesting and say hey I am watching a ghost show in the other room if you're interested and very calmly he agrees. As we are sitting there I have to say I am pretty sure he isn't there for my company but more less for the free beverage or maybe in his mind beverages but that didn't matter to me at all and to be honest I welcomed the intrusion. We talked primarily about the show that was on and he seemed to dig it and about how nice it was outside today. Bobby said he liked to barbecue and today would be a great day for it and I was like excellent why not. First though I realized we were going to need more beverages and I really didn't want to walk into the abyss so a light bulb went off over my head to just drive there and limit being out in the open.

So after getting back from the liquor store I see bobby out on the porch stoking the grill which wasn't a full grill. Well it was the part of the grill that you cooked on, however it had no legs so he placed it on this cement type post that came out of the ground just before his porch. The cement object coming out of the ground was really random and I asked Bobby if he knew what it was for. Bobby said he didn't know nor did he care let's drink and be merry. Well upon looking at the containers Bobby had the chicken in and the tools he was using I could tell right away that I did not want to eat this food. I mean the shit looked totally dirty and the chicken I was curious to know if it actually was chicken or if it was even still edible.

Of course the grilling didn't start right off the bat Bobby had to you know get the coals started and to the right color and all that, probably to make more time for drinking I thought. Man how am I going to get out of eating this food that for all I know has ten different types of bacteria on it that will render me terribly sick. Aha! I came up with the solution, get him drunk and fast. The only problem with that solution was that Bobby didn't let anyone tell him what to do and to be honest it was a nice day out and I too wanted to enjoy it so I passed on that and said to myself just flow with it.

The day went off pretty well a few crack heads passed by us and the site was appalling how skinny and sick they looked. The occasional old car retrofitted with huge oversized rims and music blaring the bass would go by. In some way it was kind of relaxing for me coming from an environment where people were for the most part well to do and had very minor concerns this made me feel almost to some extent a bit well off and not having the feeling of being less than to some extent. Although those feelings went through me I also realized the sense of total despair and apathy that pervaded these people and the neighborhood that sat patiently yet loudly seem to reinforce that atmosphere of nothing here. Bobby was doing his usual scream or shout out if you will to the neighborhood by now and I could tell that the grilling probably would not be done and that gave me a huge sigh of relief as I didn't want to offend him.

With that obstacle coming to an end I thought Bobby said all of a sudden that he needed to go inside and get the spices and marinade for the chicken. As he stumbled inside his place I followed him in to render any assistance and as I did I noticed that he was pissing in his sink! Oh my lord, I was shocked and also found it terribly humorous and with a half amazed nervousness I just laughed and went back outside. Well Bobby comes outside with some spray bottle and a few containers and said, "man I'm gonna hook this up for you this will be great". How do I get out of this? What possible excuse can I come up with? So I use an excuse that I think he would not find all too unbelievable and say that I am too drunk and have to go sleep a bit. Genius man because it worked he didn't mind in fact he said more for himself and that encounter was interesting and I remember thinking to myself that I would not eat Bobby's home cooking if at all avoidable.

About a week later I had another session with Bobby and asked him about this bar that I noticed on the block and asked whether it was a good place to go to. Bobby was right back into his somewhat racial innuendo's and said, "You cannot go there it's a black folk's bar". Again I was a bit bent out of shape with this comment as for the past week me and bobby would have drinks together on occasion and I felt that if he could hang out with me and he is black why can't I go there? Well again, he was adamant about it and basically gave me the feeling that we weren't really friends or even close to that yet and I proceeded to leave him be as I was in no mood for this shit.

The bar looked almost like a strip club to me with pink neon lights on the outside, and wings, ribs, and drinks also boasting the pink illumination. To me personally I was getting extremely tired of sitting in my cell if you will and drinking myself wet, meaning pissing myself at night. Indeed Bobby and I both were hitting the bottle hard trying to push the environment we were currently in aside and erase the one that came in our past. I was bothered of sorts with him and his obvious anger, but I said fuck it I am not a bologna sandwich I am six foot one and weigh a decent one hundred ninety five pounds. I figured I would be alright at this establishment so long as like Bobby said I watch how I conduct myself.

Friday came around quickly as most days for me were a total blur and in some cases the only way I new what day it actually was, was to turn on the direct TV that the landlady included in our rent to see the date and time. I should also say it is interesting when I conjure up the idea of myself once pretty far bent that I am like someone in the sopranos and I am going to dress nicely when going out and that people are going to think I am some kind of big shot or even better a bit on the shady side. I find myself funny at times with this because if ever I did bring home a woman she would see that I am a total loser with no great car, house, or for that matter no real money or power. But what the hell right what the hell do I have to lose, I have lost everything anyway and wanted to get out a bit more and embrace the area get some new experiences because I am no pussy.

With the beer and cigs already purchased I started on my campaign to think of myself as a somebody and figure I can tie a good one on and then go to the bar. I start to feel the effects and also like a spin of a dime Lee needs music some dance or perhaps disco. Direct TV has these channels that Bobby let me know of that have pure music all different types of genres and once I knew that I was my own d.j. I usually preferred to kick the night off with easy listening soft rock as I pondered my meek world and tried to enjoy the beers and smokes. Phil Collins in the air tonight was a big favorite of mine I really enjoy that song not many others of his but that one hits me just right. Now things are going good I have picked my attire out for my night time excursion and being satisfied I turn the dial to some disco channel and start to really enjoy myself. I like disco and dance music most heterosexual men are to macho for that and need to listen to like death metal. Unfortunately most straight men are very simple and boring people I like to compare these assholes to rocks their there but their not. In fact these types of bastards make me want to beat the shit out of something. I know I should continue the typical night by night lead up but this actually is what I would be thinking at the time.

Yeah the macho manly man who once he finds a piece of ass is a total pussy. Yet me being the I would like to think maybe metro sexual man to some extent I have to deal with their bullshit all the time primarily because men deal with men differently no matter if they are married or not, they are always tough guy douche bags around each other. Anyway after the rage analysis that often pops into my head is triggered by certain things I am comforted with the self affirmation that at least I can be multi faceted and like different music. I can talk to men and women about serious deep issues and I am not a total macho man douche bag or that's at least how I perceive myself.

Alright that felt fantastic to get off my chest indeed it did, but I am sure that mantra will be repeated as well as many others throughout this book. Well I am starting to realize as I sit Indian style on the air mattress on the floor that I am well on my way to getting really bent as I see a ring of cans surrounding me. I usually like to get pretty far gone when going out which actually would hamper any attempt to actually have a good conversation with a woman, but hey lets be honest my primary goal is to be in my own world so to speak.

As I am getting dressed I start to feel a bit uneasy and realize that my stomach is not agreeing with the fifteen beers already consumed and I have to get into my Zen mind pond and save them from expulsion. Usually what works well for me is to concentrate on the night to come and grab my stomach with a very hard grip and pinch it till it hurts taking my mind from the sick feeling to pain: works like a charm. Anyway it is time now and I have passed that little dilemma and being dressed to kill as I like to think I am off to the bar.

To get to the bar I walk through the alleyway and as I am I don't really care about the surroundings in fact I feel ten foot and bullet proof. As I enter the bar there is two big I mean big black bouncer types there and they start to frisk me as to see if I am carrying a weapon. This has never happened to me before at any bar that I have ever gone to in my whole entire life and I am thinking to myself that this white boy might be a fish in a barrel. I mean I usually understand that most bars actually have a coat check not a gun check. Well that is over I enter up some stairs and to the left is the entire bar in front of me. There was a sea of black folks seeming to be well dressed and enjoying the sounds of the evening that the d.j is playing. The bartenders ask with a almost look of seeing a ghost, "what'll you have sweetie?", I too am a bit on edge but when in Rome right so I order a jack and coke as if it is needed.

With drink in hand I look around more trying to find my scene and a seat upon I may sit to scan the hopefully hot women here. There is a small dance floor to the rear of the place with a second bar area and seating that I see offers some good viewing so off I am. I don't mind the music much and no body seems to be bothering me at all if anything I am getting the attention of the sisters there and they seem to like what they see with a smile here and a laugh there in my direction. Now I love black women always have think they are very sexy and I am always amazed at the fact that many black men seem to have this addiction to white women when I think the black woman are like tony the tiger says on frosted flakes grrrrreat! As the night progresses I also am getting pretty bombed and with a few conversations here and there I start back home as I don't want to come off too pompous or stupid.

The next morning I wake in a sea of urine this is not uncommon for me as it does happen often and if any of you say I never have pissed myself I say to you that you haven't drank enough then. With that all over my mattress I get up and hit the shower. The bathroom is not much of anything a basic tub with a shower head and toilet. What do I care I have been living in filth for awhile now and don't mind it much kind of makes me feel like Rocky in Rocky one or at least I like to think that. After the shower I feel somewhat clean and rejuvenated and decide I must get out and be productive today. First on the agenda probably should be to get some food because all I have is beer and condiments in the fridge and then secondly look for work. Buying food to me is a chore just like getting gas I fucken hate it, basically I hate it because I never really have much cash to buy anything with and I always seem to see the people with full carts and a look of not a care in the world on their face drives me nuts.

My shopping list today will consist of the usual suspects Mac and cheese Kraft though of course, milk, and penne pasta with a jar of mushroom alfredo damn it's a good meal. With that done I leave to the library and the anticipation grows that I might just might find something of value there as far as a job, my optimism is getting a standing eight count however I still try to be positive. Most of the jobs I find are sales type shit and screw sales like anyone anyway in this economy is going to buy anything right. Besides sales its all these fake job postings that staffing agencies put up there trying to catch another fish, and of course the higher end positions like health care that I am not even qualified or interested in. Fuck this why try anymore pops into my head, what's that oh it was the optimism I was barely hanging on to going right out the window.

I get the paper on a regular basis always on Sundays and I have three so called staffing agencies working for me supposedly and there isn't shit man. Ding I have a light bulb go off in my head. I haven't checked in and asked these asshole staffing douche bags if they have found anything for me recently, I mean usually they call you, but I am bored, nursing a horrible hangover, and tight with rage. Getting the phone book I look under staffing agencies as I know I marked the three with a pen when calling them initially setting up the account with them. Before I call I try to come up with my plan of attack, you know be calm, collected and professional.

CHAPTER 3

It was a sunny day out again today and before I made my call I figured I should grab a brewski and sit out on the porch with the comfortable white lawn chair that is locked to the rail of the porch, hell yeah. The first company comes through after a few rings and I start to inquire giving them name and info and politely asking for some jobs and asking why they haven't called about something to offer me. Some bitch on the other line is giving me some serious fucken attitude and my rage is almost ready to come out, she is saying, "well sir we have a lot of applicants and there just isn't that many positions that are coming to us you need to have more patience". What the fuck? Ok if I haven't made it already clear I have been unemployed now for five months and I have been patient with these idiots because they have had my resume now for two full months and this is my only inquiry to them to see the status of how things are going and this lady is really ragging it. Anyway with much self control I say thank you and hang up.

The next call I am telling myself that maybe the next call will be better trying to in some way not lose it. Like I said earlier in the book it sucks not being anybody with no power or way to get peoples attention to helping you. I swear sometimes I just want to grab the next person that gives me attitude and beat the shit out of them. On to the next call and this call ends up pretty bad. So the second company I call I actually have this guy I have been talking to once in awhile through email so I am hopeful again. I start to talk to him and he is like the same thing nothing coming up for which I would qualify, and I get aggravated and start to say, "what the hell do you guys do then can I work there since it seems there is no staffing being done can I sit on my ass and get paid too?". Well that didn't go over well and he in return got aggressive and with that I let him meditate to the dial tone click.

The final and third call to the excellent staffing agencies in Milwaukee goes from bad to worse. The lady I talked to this time just makes me feel like a total impotent, worthless pussy of a man. I mean I ask her the same shit and still polite though and she's like telling me basically that my resume isn't up to snuff, that I need to do this and that and to just shut up and we will call you. Like a pissed off black woman or gay black man, "oh no she didn't!" That's it now this company the last one on the list I have actually called and left messages for the person handling my resume to call me back to discuss and none of my calls have ever been returned so this is even more fuel to my fire. So I go look here woman, "I have called your rep many times and left messages with nothing not an email back or simple call to acknowledge me", then I really went nuts, "what do I have to do come down there and talk to you people personally?" She didn't like that but fuck it I was on a mission to at least be acknowledged, so I say "screw it shred my info and take me off your damned companies listing" then click I hang up.

It was a boiling point for me I am trying to find work on my own finding jack shit and hoping against all hope it turned out that these companies would be assisting me and they had nothing. I was upset because I wasn't being even treated in a courteous way initially not before today obviously but to the two companies that it went bad with I mean no email return or a simple call saying we are working on this hang in there, that would have satisfied me personally. Well a few hours later I get a call from the Glendale police department regarding one of the

25

staffing agencies I guess that works out of that suburb. Much to my amazement some bitch called the cops worried that I indeed would come down there and do what, a mass killing? I told the officer to chill and that I wasn't meaning any harm but told him I was merely voicing my frustrations with them and my current situation. That seemed to please him and that was that, but boy I tell you this country and these people are fucken pissing me off, I mean that lady couldn't take some anger, I never said anything about violence what a bunch of pussies. Nevertheless, life and these situations have taught me after reviewing these moments a few revelations upon which I was searching for.

First of all as I am sure this will not sound like a revelation to most is that you are on your own. That you and only you are totally responsible for your life and your survival. Now I am sure many will say in a rebuttal that there is plenty of people around I am sure that will help you out, but I have experienced that in life there is self reliance or the street. I really started to realize in these last few months that I am truly on my own. On my own for financial support, on my own for emotional support, and basically alone on my spiritual front. I look at people that are self sufficient and married or what have you and am amazed. It seems that I do not or cannot have that type of determination. I have really never known how it feels to be taken care of in the true sense. So I guess as I write this it is a bit mind blowing that I have just came to this idea or revelation if you will.

I think in part a lot of it had to do with the fact of being busy all the time. I started working at age fifteen and never really have been unemployed or had so much time to myself ever in my life to reflect on the fact that all I have really is my own self. I think in life or at least mine I will not pull a Dr. Phil on any of you reading this, that we are occupied so much of the time with this or that and once if given the time to reflect and meditate on ones own life we come to this very conclusion. For example, take the previous story I just described about the staffing agencies and their total incompetence in my mind to even offer me a position of worth or give me the time of day. I often am exhausted at the fact of my own friends and family and the lack of communication and dialogue I have with them. Many of my male friends, women do not count because they are pretty self involved anyway, once married or in a serious relationship I never hear from them again. Kiss that long friendship goodbye because they are too busy or are in that routine the work life the marriage, kids, or what have you. I came to find that at least in my experience I am always the one no matter if working or not is always the one that for the most part makes the first call, email, or howdy do on the street. And after thirty years of this I finally came to the realization of, "do not expect shit from anyone".

This notion of being on your own and not trusting I think would be a good word to interject here on anyone hasn't been my mere pessimism it has been taught to me through countless experiences and friendships including my family. As I came to this realization I was sitting on the air mattress by myself looking through my phone at all the recent calls that were received and saw that it would take a shocking two and sometimes almost three months until I heard from people. I can never and will never understand the person that I stood at for their wedding as best man telling me that they are too busy for an email or phone call, again the staffing agency response; however from a long time friend it burns. I think the comment I was too busy or am too busy should in fact be like a bubble over that persons head like in a comic book really reading, "Fuck off". Anyway I will get back to this more I am sure, but I want to touch on a few other thoughts that came into my mind after that appalling go fuck yourself I received from the staffing agencies.

Second what I also found with their almost script like responses to me about why I wasn't getting calls or any attention regarding job placement was that people tell you what they think they should say or what they have heard rammed into them countless times before. Basically, what I mean by this is that I have found that when in most cases seeking advice or counsel from a friend

27

or family member I get this regurgitation of diarrhea shit. You know the half assed response that you would expect from say a passer by on the street if talking about your life and them giving you some thoughtless almost zombie like response. Or the total asshole person who always gives you the, "it could be worst", comment or, "you need to be more positive" shit.

Whatever happened to real dialogue? Real concern? God forbid real insight and wisdom? Again it goes back to the Americans total lack of time and zombie like self involvement. I recently witnessed this documentary on suburban life and how fucked up it is and it really struck me about our country. It showed a bunch of people actually I think in Canada, however the sickness of a schedule and all that comes with that can infect any society I imagine. It showed how these communities were set up in such a way that discouraged actual community. It showed how the garages faced out to the street sending a clear passive aggressive message of leave us the fuck alone. How cookie cutter the buildings were with no real character or at least that's what I have always thought to myself when driving on the freeway and witnessing them.

They had people on this movie that clearly were giving you the script they heard from the shallow, ditsy, money grubbing real estate agent it was amazing. You know the neighborhood is nice even though eighty percent of it was still under construction and filled with hazard chemicals all waiting for little Johnny and Jane to get right into it. The it's a good school district type of mundane make me yawn comments. However I didn't hear of the neighbors are great or my child had good people to play with.

I just cannot believe the degree in which people have really turned into themselves and I feel not in a positive way. With the advent of the internet, cell phones, and all of that the person has had to not rely on inter personnel skills and communication and is now almost like a script, a zombie, or the preverbal message that play on any type of customer service line that comes on when trying to get through to either your cable company or phone company. It really pisses me off that I feel like I am starting to hate people now. I find them to be oh so very trivial and to some extent simplistic to the point of madness. The typical American who almost brags about the fact in which they work sixty hour weeks or more! Are you fucking kidding me that is something to basically be proud off? Whatever happened to Ward and June Cleaver, because today's world is nothing even remotely like that. I hope I didn't lose anyone with any of this it is just that as I sit here I realize that whether it be calling a staffing agency or a friend or family member that I get the same mundane talk and to some extent silence and it really makes me think and question to some extent what is this experience really telling in a verbal sense or showing me visually?

Man another day and I received a very interesting call from a long time friend I made back in Ann Arbor. Kevin L. was not in a good mood as life has been beating the shit out of him as well. He started talking about the lack of tang acquisition, or rather getting laid. How difficult it was in this country compared to Panama where he went on a vacation recently. I started to laugh and of course instantly sympathized with his plight. Now I in general also to let you know am not a big fan of the American women and how ridiculous they have become. I started to tell him that I agreed, but also was not putting the tang as we called it first anymore it was just too much of a rage factor for me.

Kevin indeed agreed with that but didn't want to here that instead he goes off on how he sees all these fine women with total douche bag looking men. I interjected with a huge applause and my explanation for why he was seeing this horrible image time and time again. I said in essence that most American women could careless what you look like but do care what your bank account looks like. They could care less if you have a small penis just as long as you had cash. Kevin L. found this to be very true in his thinking as well and also let out a huge Uh!, as to show his profound appreciation for my comments.

I also wanted to discuss with him in general the amount of labor it takes to keep an American spoiled lazy woman these days. The amount of time and energy a male must pour into this tang acquisition effort is something I don't think women today appreciate. I started to tell Kevin how the few male friends I have known through the years once dating or married are virtual prisoners and no longer heard from again. Kevin being once married now divorced sighed as to prepare his thoughts and rebuttal. Kevin said that he knew that was right, but that was one thing that hindered his relationship with his wife was the fact of total suffocation and no time to himself. He went on to tell of how she wanted to do this or that and watch this or that, and him trying to be accommodating tried with great effort to keep up but couldn't. Going on he said how a man needs to have his space as well as a woman needs to have her space.

Such music to my ears as he went on as he is probably one of two guys that I talk to that seem to have this idea and total belief. I said to him as I will echo many times I am sure in this novel that American men are plain beat up pussies to the tang. American married men are a total nosebleed and I go on to say to him the idea of how having a conversation with one especially if you are unmarried is very unnerving. Kevin again recited an Uh! This aspect of our society and how men are treated like shit by most of their so called wives or girlfriends is like a virus spreading through television and stupid women magazines.

Now I am sure there might be a few women reading this just ready to scream that men do treat women poorly and this is not at all a one sided argument, my answer to them is to wake the hell up and be real here because this isn't meant to please everyone as it is my book and point of view.

Anyway with that disclaimer being put out there Kevin goes on to say that he is very frustrated and that him being a well built man with muscles and a decent look cannot manage any women at all. For not the first time but rather the thousandth time I say to him a quote many of us know, "it's all about the

Benjamin's baby". I have to end the call with him as my rage grows never really needing a push or shove these days and reflect on my thoughts and feelings.

Well I should probably only discuss my experiences or how I perceive them to be instead of making generalizations, it will be hard but I shall try. Now I know it might sound chauvinistic of me to mention this but I would like to mention the show Leave it to Beaver for starters. You know June the good wholesome stay at home mom making sure Ward and the kids have the food and everything else they desire. The reason I am bringing this up is because today that image is not only over it is smashed. And to some extent that's good being that women have the right to do whatever their hearts desire, but women I have met for the most part do not, cannot, or will not make a nice meal for their man, or treat him respectfully and instead yell at them and treat them including myself like we are merely a means to an end for their lives. The workplace really pounds this notion home for me.

At every single job that I have ever worked at there are always quite a few women who do nothing but bad mouth their men. In one instance I was surrounded by four women in a cubicle environment and I felt violated. They were saying how lazy their men are, how they are not sensitive enough, how they don't make enough money ad nauseum. Finally after months of hearing these woman bitch I stood up and said hey I am a man here can you keep the man hating down? They looked at me with that witchy look and kept right on: I was astounded. Picture this double standard a bunch of men doing the exact same thing in a work environment calling their women fat, lazy, and stupid, you think that would be tolerated I think not.

In America today this is rampant this double standard to the point of making me want to vomit. Also at most of my previous jobs I hear the excuse that is always I mean always used in a snotty way when describing why they were late, leaving early, or in a bad mood its, "my kids" excuse. Now I am sure that it is indeed a valid excuse sometimes but I have seen the same women use it several times a month over and over again. I guess this really pissed me off because I am single and I cannot use that excuse as bullshit to get out of being reprimanded for tardiness or bad performance. I think no I know there are a lot of men that are silent with this and do not state their rage but I am not like most and this story is about cleansing my mind.

Enough said about that but I think I have let you all know that the workplace is a great way to see how women are in some cases taking advantage of their sex. On to the sexier part of what Kevin got me thinking of and that is relationships. I have been burned every single damn time with my relationships. I swear I must have cheat on me tattooed to my forehead. I was a sensitive man and still like to think of myself as one but after getting the shit kicked out of me and having my heart roasted a few times that is very difficult for me to still do. I think like I stated before it is that money and greed has really made many American women very shallow and quick to leave relationships. The bbd or bigger better deal as I call it complex. Now in all my relationships I never made much money I wasn't poor but I just couldn't seem to keep up with the womanly demand for this or that and the women that left me left no room for interpretation they basically said they want to go and travel and have nice things. I believe that be a major reason why many would cheat on me or leave me because I wasn't well to do, now I am sure many are saying to themselves right now, "lee you do seem like an asshole though", well I wasn't born that way these women made me that way as well as many other things.

Speaking of assholes, many of my first relationships started off when I treated them like shit. Can you believe that? Yes American women that I have dated and seen date others I know seem to like that to some extent. Eventually though they would get to see that I wasn't an asshole and when I treated them nicely boom they seem to lose interest and of course cheat on me for the BBD, bigger better deal. I just find women to be very contradictory, I mean the I am women hear me roar type once pregnant want to sit on their ass at home and not work. The women that tell me and many that they are just looking for a nice guy and all that but date the wife beater guy amaze me as well. The woman that says money isn't important, c'mon man now that one is just plain funny. I really don't know but I have been overseas and the women I met there were down to earth nice simple women, American women are such high maintenance it's exhausting.

I know there has to be good women out there but they just don't make them like June Cleaver anymore and to be quite honest I think the quality of American women has gone down like the stock market here in 2008. I love when I hear the rebuttal of women that say we are equal and all that. Well I just have seen and heard a lot from them that makes me come to the conclusion that their bodies might have matured but their minds and emotional state is like that of a child still. I mean they cry over not being able to open a can at work right in front of everyone, they can be openly depressed or down and have time to deal with it, they can shop for cute shoes and gossip about each other like in grade school, sheesh. Yes I am women hating a bit aren't I? Well cant I? It is funny if I were a women writing this portion about men I would be on Oprah with great praise and acknowledgement for being empowered what a crock. Oh well right, I mean be in the now Lee do not expect much in the form of nurturing or loving behavior from your women just make money come home and shut the fuck up, and if you don't and you are married she will get the kids, your house, your car, your pension, half your social security and shit maybe even your soul.

That felt great to get off my chest. I am sure I will have more to add throughout and sound redundant, but I am writing to you as this is an ongoing conversation. I am not trying to hit on one thing in chapter one and then another in two, whatever is going on in my life like Kevin's call that brought this up or the staffing agencies I am going to touch on it, and I hope you all can handle that and follow the story.

CHAPTER 4

The night has come and after discussing this I could use a drink. The rain is starting to fall outside which I do not mind because it matches my emotional state right now. I heard Bobby in the other room yelling again, great. I look into the fridge of filth and see I am out of beers and I know I must go downtown to my shopping place and procure a few dozen. I grab my coat as it is fall and the weather is a bit nippy. As I am driving to my destination I turned on the radio I usually listen to a rock station no hip hop crap for me I hear enough in the hood here anyway. With cigarette in my left hand I open the window a bit and turn up the volume on my radio. Oh my goodness it cannot be this song which is one of my favorites, I believe it is by Cinderella the song goes, "you don't know what you got till it's gone". I am not sure of the actual title or if it is by Cinderella but it's hitting me right where it needs to right now. Reminding me of all the women that have gone and left me and the fact to some extent that I am starting to figure out what that terrible feeling that was brewing inside me was.

The street lights from overhead are creating nice shadows in my car along with the cigarette smoke. The song I turn up all the way and enjoy it to the fullest. As I approach downtown Milwaukee with the skyline in view it almost feels like I should be in a movie of sorts, or at least that's what I imagine to myself. That sick feeling again re-enters my mind and soul the music acting as a switch releasing the emotions. I pull into the marketplace and sit there in my car with the rain pelting it unmercifully. I need to finish my smoke and as I listen to the song I am overcome by a relentless feeling of total abandonment. I am looking at people going into the store together and having some sort of companionship and as I steam up my windows with the cigarette smoke and the humidity induced by my heat and the rain I feel totally alone.

Beers being bought I seek the refuge of my domicile. When I get back inside I can hear that Bobby is in not rare form but the usual. A lot of music blaring and a bit of yelling is to let me know Bobby might want some company this dreary evening. So I put away the beers and unload my coat and other non essentials and go knock on Bobby's door. I soon realize that it is going to take awhile to get his attention given the noise that is being produced so I am cracking my beer preparing for a few minute wait. Finally Bobby comes to the door and once opening it a whirl of wind and music floods my being. Bobby is quite pleased to see me and I ask him if I may enter his domicile and slam a few cold ones with him. Bobby is very welcoming and to my amazement his place is almost spotlessly clean. As I walk in I see the old boom box that I have seen previously outside when I hung out with him playing on a chair. He has a bed an actual bed unlike myself that was made up and looked and seemed to be very clean. I must admit after the first encounter with him when I went to walk inside and saw him pissing in the sink I was shocked that his place was very well taken care of.

We started to talk about the weather and how the rain was really coming down this evening and I was instantly put to ease and in some sense really could tell that this was a good man at heart. The television that he had was in poor shape all the colors were obviously not the right colors that they were intended to be but hey he has TV right. I also noticed a lot of clothes hanging up on these racks and they all seemed again to be clean and neatly organized. Now I am starting to think to myself that this man has not only substance but is going to probably teach me more than I am going to teach him, but still I hope I can teach him a few things as well. The conversation continued and we began to talk about the music he was listening to and how he liked it. I cannot recall the actual names of the groups but he let me know they were old school as he called it. With the music playing, beer flowing, and the rain it set an interesting mood to say the least.

I started to really feel at peace inside that I haven't felt in almost a year. I started to actually relax and live in the now and not worry about all the troubles that were possessing my mind. I took a match and lit a smoke and pulled hard on my beer and looked at bobby and said, "Hey man at least we are not homeless right?" Bobby was like, "hell yeah playa we got all we need right here man". That was very interesting to me and being that I have been in a very dark and negative mood lately it was like lotion being put on a bad sunburn, it soothed me. As the night went on and the rain fell even harder the satellite that we gained our cable through began to sporadically break up and leave just the music and us together. I started to ask him about his background you know the typical, where you from, do you have kids shit like that. Bobby was more than receptive to my inquiry and gave me all the information that I wanted to know. He had a few kinds a few marriages and came from Arkansas, but had family up here.

The visit reminded me of the first time that we spent time together outside on that front porch. The sun was shining and starting to go down and it seemed like there was a peace around that was there but could not be seen. The simplicity of him and now my existence was in some way starting to make me feel less constrained. As we sat there I felt very at ease and just relaxing with Bobby kicking in a few "yeeeohhh's" to bring a brilliant smile to my face, a face that has only seen tears and sadness lately. Yes these first few visits were a welcomed experience and I really needed that tonight. After thinking of my loneliness and lack of female companionship it felt nice to be in the company of another lost soul. I guess it is true misery loves company.

After a few hours went by Bobby said he had to go to bed and as he hobbled his way to the refrigerator to put a half drunk beer in I got up and said, "Thanks man it was great we should do this again sometime". Bobby with a smile and nod reaffirmed to me that would be the case in the future. When I got back into my apartment the loneliness started to really sink in again. I guess it is just very hard for me recently to be alone; everyday that passes is like another notch of the effects of isolation that hurt me. And as I said earlier the feeling that I was trying to put my finger on was starting to come very clear to me as if I was once looking at a mirror after a shower and now I have wiped it clean.

The feeling that I think has been troubling me so very much is the feeling of losing all optimism and hope for my future. The fact that I am really starting to realize what kind of pathetic state not only I am in but also the country the total apathy and loathing that is in no short supply. I have often felt very alone in life and never really felt that I belonged to anyone or anything and I guess in some way I was not aware of the tragic effects that has once one comes to the conclusion that you are indeed on your own and shit just keeps coming your way. I mean even in the darkest of my moments in life I now look back and see that I was very optimistic and still believed that there would be something for me in this life: I cannot say that anymore today. I look at the fact as I have said earlier that I cannot find a decent job that will not only support me but god forbid a family if I was to so choose. The American ideal of working a job and supporting yourself let alone children to me is infinitely dead and over.

I sit here staring at the cigarette smoke being made apparent by the dim light I have in my kitchen area and these thoughts or the revelation of my loss of optimism or maybe in some way the actual loss of my innocence or ignorance at age thirty appalls me severely. My god I think to myself as I pull very hard on this beer and cigarette, what am I going to do? I mean I really feel as if I have lost my soul in some regards in these last few months, my dignity, my aspirations, my hope. I sit here and ponder my dreary situation as the alcohol starts to reengage my senses and let me know that I do not have to worry to hard about that right now, however I cannot shake it and I am to some extent proud of myself for realizing that I have lost my hope but also very troubled as well.

Fuck it! This is too much for me to handle right now and my emotional status is at the very best very unstable. I notice a tear coming down my cheek and I start to hyperventilate and am soon on the floor in a terrible state. The I am macho man fuck it shit isn't working at this moment and I am very terrified at the prospects of how I can even help myself? After the tears subside a bit I grab another beer because to be honest it is all I have really and it is my only friend. I started to think about how I could even get back that eye of the tiger so to speak like in Rocky. How can I become again the optimistic American worker bee looking at a positive future? This is not going to happen and I want not to believe this but I have to. That I am in some way very wounded by a lot of the shit going on now and in the past.

With beers flowing down my throat like the raging Mississippi in a flood I remove myself from these feelings. Put on the television be numb in that sense that is what I do and turn it to the music channels and then go sit on my front porch and stare at the walking dead passing by, the sirens of police going near by, and the smell of urine that punctuates this moment even more for my senses. It was a nice night with the rain coming down and the cloud cover ahead it painted a very nice somber tone to this movie I am in. Sitting there I just tried to zone out and not think of what I was earlier and live in the moment as so many people say we should do. Yes live in the moment another terrible cliché that I wish I could say I do enthusiastically. Nevertheless, the neighborhood started to produce some very interesting entertainment for me, the crack heads passing by, the cops, and of course the local stray cat brigade that was always hunting in the trash bins.

In some way I just concentrated on the activities around me and it made me feel very numb something I was desperately in need of at that time. I have to be numb in this moment of my life or I might snap something I come to understand also here. The lack of hope and optimism about ones own future is devastating to the mind and spirit and it is better to medicate with alcohol or drugs at least that is the prescription I have given unto myself. Man I am in some serious need of a huge hug and cry however they are in short supply upon my spirits demand. As I sit in this plastic chair in the night air and smell the rain I do not feel any company with me. Yes, indeed I am starting to question also my faith and all the bullshit that has been crammed down my throat by people who are less than desirable as far as moral teaching is concerned, or at least that's what I think anyway.

Everything is in question now at this period in my life and nothing is left unturned. Religion and all that comes with that is burdening my heart like an anchor sinking to the bottom of the ocean. I don't know is that okay? I don't know about my future and what I want or who I even am at this stage in my life, is that okay? It is over, is all that repeats through my mind like a CD that has a scratch and is skipping repeatedly. I see people on television and they seem to be very concrete in their beliefs and life. I guess if I was on television I also would not be to concerned with much as I would assume I would be making good money. I do not know as I sit here and smoke and drink in this very dreary atmosphere and ponder like Poe my future. Also my past I come to the realization that it is indeed over. What I mean by that is that my mental thinking of how things are to be is over in a gigantic way for me.

I am alone. The friends that I have are for the most part very casual and fleeting, and soon as they find a woman or whatever the fuck they are searching for I hear and see them no more. I want to scream and say dammit, "I hurt, and am totally lost and pissed off", but I know that no one is listening or for that matter really honestly gives a flying shit. I wish as I sit here I could be a worker bee drone that most of us have turned into or have been turned into by this shitty capitalistic society. I wish I could look at a woman and be instantly turned on by her appearance and also not needing an intelligent discussion from her. Man my anger is so immense it scares me silent. I want to be productive and self loving, but how can one do that when they honestly have never felt that before in life? I guess I want to write this novel because I want to get out my feelings, thoughts, and experiences to all of you before I die. I feel that I am on borrowed time in some way and want to make my impact before it is too late. Yes, love and all that comes with it, I have been burned before but as I look back these women and myself were not mature enough to be in love in the first place.

The rain is starting to saturate me and I enter back into my domicile thinking hard on these thoughts. When I enter in I look around and ponder the dilemma I am in. I need to grab another beer and smoke and at least for those few minutes I am un bothered by my thinking. The crack of the beer and the sizzle of the cigarette once I light it and pull hard on it is interesting. With a blood alcohol content that is more than likely well over the limit I enter my side room and play some music. Recently I have been listening to a lot of Annie Lennox music, the Diva CD to be exact. I also listened to that CD a lot when I was back in Ann Arbor doing a lot of cocaine. As I sit their and listen to the first track on the album, which is titled. "Why", I smile and in some sort of way say to myself isn't this song appropriate to the situation.

The song is very somber and hits me not only in my heart but also my thinking. Why is this my place in society and life right now? Why am I in such desperation and loathing? I often wonder these things as I am sure you the reader have obviously concluded. I guess I want a lot out of life and not to be merely surviving through this dance. I want to be loved, to be important to someone or some people, I want to believe, and I want to feel that people are inherently good at the bottom of it. Indeed I know this is like many people have said to me asking a lot to ask out of life and people, but then why the fuck exist? I am not perfect and I am not saying that others have to be, however I want more out of this life than what I am living in! Here I am just amazed at how in our society some have gotten a good hand while others have busted. The people that have that great hand tell those that have busted to suck it up and not complain.

I in some way am thankful for this suffering I am in and have gone through so that it allows me to look at those less fortunate in a compassionate way. I wish those that had that winning hand could also do that, unfortunately the sad truth is that you as a person can not relate to that which you do not know. Also I think the sad truth to that those are the same people who are currently running this warped society. It is over, my rage is welling up even more than usual and I want to scream yet like I said before no one will listen to me. Why? The song continues to play and now finally the tears are starting to well up on my eyelids. I sit silently holding back the gasping of air that I am searching for because I am starting to break down and cry. The cigarette in my hand is almost burning my fingers and the beer now almost warm, yet I do not care. I let the song proceed and come to the conclusion that I am seriously burdened by these thoughts and yet I do not know what to do about it.

CHAPTER FIVE

The night went and as this morning comes to life I lay on this half inflated air mattress staring at the ceiling. My body is feeling like road kill and my thoughts are only on water and how much money and beer I have left. With piss in a puddle around my waist my skin is wrinkled as I stand up with great difficulty I realize that the night before I must have punched something again as my hand is very swollen. Reminds me of a phone conversation I had a few days ago with my father. I tried to tell him along with my mother of the pain and suffering I was going through and to no avail. I got the quick response like well keep trying and let's talk about the weather from him and most people I try to dialogue with. I guess that is what brought up the whole aspect of nobody wants to experience and know pain to me. My hand hurts but who knows really what that feels like until they smash their own hand into something in a fit of rage.

I guess I too have lost the capacity as it is to bullshit. I think that is what many of us do in our day to day lives. If I cannot even be honest with my parents who can I be honest with? I started to think of all the times I really needed guidance and teaching as a young man and almost dropped to my knees at the realization that shit it just wasn't there. I guess in a lot of ways my parents have also lost the capacity to feel and love. My parents were providers in the sense of housing and food but in the sense of nurturing boy were they absent! I guess this morning I started to look at my hand and want someone to blame for this physical pain and my emotional pain. I got very pissed off and realized again that I am alone in this struggle of life and that my parents along with others are merely acquaintances.

So again I want the bottle at least that doesn't ignore me and make me feel less than or like a mirage that is merely seen but never touched. If maybe I had some kind of real attention I could have been more of a happy and fulfilled person. My hangover and hunger for booze along side with my intense dread lead me out the door to the liquor store to acquire some more needed medicine. As I leave I have to shut the door in a careful way as my right hand is hurting me in a very real way. I walk to the front of the house with nothing but loss in me. No body really gives a shit. I have been asking if not pleading for love, help, and understanding for quite a few years.

As I walk to the store I am accosted by a bunch of crack head bitches. Give me this and that the usual type of shit that one gets in the hood. As I am in no mood for this I try to be accommodating and say no and move on. Then one of these bitches gets in my face and starts to get quite aggressive with me. Yelling and being very insulting to me with all the walking dead able to witness this. Now to the white person that doesn't know hood living let me say that appearances are very important in the hood and if I take this shit I may be perceived as an easy mark. My rage is overwhelming and I want to beat the living shit out of these bitches and scream to all in earshot that this isn't happening anymore! I wish American women would treat men a little bit or rather a lot better. I am no slouch and stand six feet one inch and weigh around two hundred pounds, am I not a threat of beating your stupid ass? My god I am not saying or advocating the abuse of women, but Jesus, show men respect, especially if you do not know them and are not fucking them my god. Of course these were not women I mean they were but not typical women these were crack head bitches.

I pass the confrontation and proceed to gain my fix as that is all that really matters to me god forbid I beat the shit out of someone and even though in my mind I am justified I would probably go to jail. After the beer has been purchased I return through the same maze of misery that I went through before. What a shit hole I think to myself. How do people like living this way? Fuck it the apathy that this area has, has indeed infected me now at this point. I stumble back to my humble abode with plastic making noises at every bump upon by brews. I get back and the crack whores are gone and I am totally relieved. I often am challenged by people whether it be just this trying to go grab a few beers or at the supermarket and I want to let them all know that I am allowing you another day today. My rage is scary and I find that I am very close to doing great bodily harm to those that want to challenge me because in some respects I have nothing to lose. What lose my freedom? If one doesn't have the resources and means to move or change something, aren't they already a prisoner? What is freedom in this bullshit godforsaken country anyway?

With the order completed and the day growing on I enter my domicile. With beers placed in the refrigerator and a smoke in hand I walk into my room part of the place and play some much needed music. What the fuck right play some Cinderella, "you don't know what you got till its gone", I believe I thought I said earlier that I wasn't certain if it was them but it says so on the TV. With smoke billowing out of my head like a toxic coal plant I seem to be at ease even though the crack head bitches are still making me want to grab my right hand and smash it again at some unmovable surface. What an existence man I and with the few remaining thoughts of being a normal being I go grab another one and try to in a serious way extinguish this fire in my soul. Man alive does this shit suck! I can only imagine the families in their nice suburban get the fuck out of our business houses. The dad that hates his now bitchy wife, and the wife that hates her poor non providing husband, and the children smoking grass and getting drunk because their parents are too busy hating each other and their places in life. Man I guess I do not have it that bad do I?

My god that's the American way, shit the American dream, or as I call it the American nightmare. Let us all work ourselves into complete and utter non existence. Yes these beers are hitting me right now and as I walk in a pace like manner like a man waiting his execution in one hour these are the things I think about. Why should I bitch right shit move on suck it up, love it right? Well to those Americans saying that to me right now I say to you, please enter an alley way and let us get it on!

Why cannot we be like the Native Americans and live in a communal and civilized way? Oh that is right we killed most of them and imprisoned the rest. This country is not only liable and wrong it is immoral. The Native Americans, people I think very highly of, were people that used what they needed in order to survive, nothing less nothing more. The Calvary comes and destroys a way of life that was existing for probably thousands of years. Maybe this may seem very erratic my writing and thinking but hey it isn't supposed to be perfect, yet it is supposed to be my thoughts throughout my experience here and now.

I decided I needed to walk into the library here on Martin Luther King Jr. Boulevard, with no real agenda, and as I muster some energy I guzzle the last of my bottles and slip on my flip flops. Walking there I want to hear some classical music some Johann Sebastion Bach or to make it easier to those, some Bach. I arrive at the library and I hear a lady doing some tutorial on something like Microsoft word. The lady has a pin-up or thing hanging from the wall and is reminding me of college and high school lectures. I found that I was in a waiting list for the computers and selected some Bach for my listening pleasure as I in some weird way was mesmerized by her dictation very monotone and boring yet brought something to my mind.

I thought that I wish some day somebody might give my life and this work of art that much attention. I started to reflect on my past as I often do, yet have not delved into in this novel. I started to remember the totally boring instruction that I had to put myself in especially in college to gain some sort of knowledge. Standing there witnessing this display of total boredom it in some way made me smile. The area filled up with all black folks trying to gain the computer skills supposedly needed to obtain gainful employment. With a smile and with the Bach CD in hand I have a nice smile on my face. Not a rude or discerning look no a look of amazement that was interesting to me. Her voice was very hypnotizing and standing there with the discs in hand looking I felt like a zombie. To be taught, to be able to be taught, to listen without the knowledge or questioning that this person might not be worthy of teaching me was amazing to me.

Now obviously I am already on a very good drunk and usually for me to be quiet in this state is highly unusual but in this instance it was quite natural actually. Her voice was very pleasant and nice to hear almost like a mother telling her child to go do a chore or to mind her, but with a nice smile and gentle nudge. I was interrupted in my bliss by a staffer that politely asked me, "Sir do need assistance?" I was terribly inconvenienced and irritated, yet replied, "No I am just fine thank you". I continued to stand there with some look probably on my face with my eyes being red, and by my breath reeking of booze of someone that should be at home. I wanted to remain their and listen and be taught again and to again be a student not a veteran of this life. Man how these simple life experiences can come into your life and if you are willing can make you pause like I am right now.

Drunk and with some unwanted attention starting to come my way I made my rental of Mr. Johann Sebastian Bach's music and left quickly. I wish I could have stayed there in that spot forever in some way instead of heading out that door and into the hood with the struggle of my life. I wish I was a child again. Walking back among the walking dead and with cars racing by to their bullshit so-called important destinations I am filled with the loss I wanted to ignore these so many years. Man it is not that late and I again am confronted by the clock.

The clock to many might not be much but to people like myself lately it is a prison. To many who say they do not have enough time to do the things they wish I say to them, "Too much time also is a burden". I find it interesting as I continue to walk back and with my Bach c.d's in hand I feel like there is no time but the past. Meaning that I haven't had anything in the present besides the lady teaching at the library to bring much joy or relaxation to me. Although the television is my second friend to that of alcohol lately and as I return to my place I turn on the television and see the economic meltdown that is occurring here in the end of 2008, and all the so-called solutions they are coming up with that turn my stomach.

Indeed this economic meltdown has been affecting a lot of Americans, however I am incensed when I hear that we as a society need to bail out these crooked company's like AIG and the like. Yes God forbid socialized medicine for us poor and screwed, but when it comes to Stanley at his Wall Street office and him not getting his ridiculously high bonus we should jump in and bail that water out of their boat right? I am just so sick of the way this country is going and how it is not the land of the free and that there really isn't free market opportunity to the small guys, especially the small farmers out there or the one or two holding on for dear life.

I watch these so-called analysts and all their bullshit and scream, "all of you are fricken filthy rich and have vested interest in these ridiculous bailouts!" I remember one show I was watching when the commentators were talking about once the election comes and there will be a new administration how these private sector people will leave their swank jobs and be forced to take the measly paying government jobs. How appalling, I do not know the specific pay grades for say the secretary of state or any of the others but I am assuming it is still close to around two hundred thousand dollars a year give or take twenty right. I mean what

American wouldn't be thanking their lucky stars for some kind of paying job like that and these idiots on these network shows make it seem like peanuts.

With the election coming here in a month and all the rhetoric for the usual suspects I just am waiting for the American people to stand up and get a backbone about these shitty choices and also what they are doing with regard to these bailouts. I too though am guilty of total apathy; I mean who in their right mind is going to listen to a thirty year old, unemployed loser right. Whatever happened to the sixties and the grassroots uprising that came at that time where people predominately college kids and other young people took a stand and said, "No more". I again say this is no land of the free and that most Americans feel that if they do standup they will be punished by their representatives in the government, or at least that is how I feel if you can even get a hold of your representative. It is over! That is one of my mantras lately I have been saying to my peers as we discuss the state of this so-called union. The government no longer is afraid of the people or feels that they need to really represent them and thus screws them. I mean look at these representatives they are all lawyers from great universities or at least most of them and they are all hooked in the Washington and corporate loops. After working in Wall Street they run for office or vice versa it's disgusting.

And since there is nothing being done in this time of economic melt down that seems to me to be anything resembling responsible management or care for our country's best interest I say we need to have term limits on these congressman! No longer can we have someone in office that is out of touch and making the "public service", there "self service". I really understand that this will probably never ever happen because for that to occur you would have to have these corrupt greed laden people manage themselves and pass that into law. I mean every year for the most part these guys and gals have no problem with giving themselves nice raises every year while the typical American worker barely gets a cost of living adjustment to even stay at par with inflation. It's disgusting to me plain disgusting. I mean the taxpayer or slaves that we are, are having really no real chance to do anything in our real interest. I mean just in the last twenty five years I have seen even since a little kid yes I can remember that the small town men and women and towns have been totally decimated, not only economically, but also in their confidence in their government.

For example, go ask many of your friends and even the random fellow beat down American walking down the street if they trust their government to do right by them and I would say almost certainly that many would say they do not. Again how pathetic is that after all that the typical American has sacrificed for their country to have representatives that they know are truly in some way screwing them over. Yes like Obama said many of us are very bitter and with good reason to be too! As the muck that comes out of these peoples mouths on television continues to spew and with the ticker on the lower right hand side on the bottom of the TV shows the market tumbling I smile. I start to think to myself that maybe I guess America hasn't really been flushed down the toilet yet. That maybe there is some stool still at the bottom and it needs to get messier before the American public gets off their asses and puts away the bon bons and television. Like I said I am too guilty so by no means do I want to not let that be known here.

However, it takes a grassroots ground swell to get the attention of these feudalistic lords in Washington's hearts to start to pound with a sense of urgency to do the right thing. I am often wishing for the revolt of America again. I think back to the Boston tea party event and that the American Revolution was started in part because of taxes on tea! Man would our founding fathers I am sure be disgusted at the current American leadership and her peoples lack of keeping them in check. I am so wishing for the pitchfork type action with the mob breaking down the doors and really saying, "Mr. over paid CEO we are taking what you have thank you". I see everyday recently on the news of how much these bastards are being compensated for running huge companies into the ground year after year and am appalled. Millions upon millions of dollars, I mean really people is anyone person worth that much money especially if they are failing miserably? Is the grunt worker that punches the clock everyday alongside his wife who also has to work any less valuable? Well it is sad to say that they are in our society and no one can tell me different because actions by our leaders speak louder than there bullshit lip service they give us every four or two years for their re-election bids.

The gibberish of McCain and those good ole republicans with the saying of America is great and that it is going to better for future generations? The democrats say basically the same thing too let us not forget how they are basically like the republicans in most ways. Are they seriously kidding me? I can assure them and all the American people that the generation x generation will be the first to do worst than their parents generation. It is happening right now to me and all those in that generation first hand, so when I hear that garbage coming out of their mouths I am just amazed that these are the two parties and the two men we have to vote for and have no damn clue to what is happening for the up coming Americans.

Oh well right let us not despair and hope right. Well all I can say is I do not want your tired clichés and your tired outdated rhetoric, just fix the damn problems! Unfortunately like most empires that have come and gone throughout history there usually is a time limit on how long they exist for. I believe that our empire doesn't have much longer to go on with this path these idiots have chosen to put us on. It is over for us and that is why I felt that would be a title for this book, "it's over". I just do not feel apart of this country and do not feel I have a real vested interest in it anymore either. I mean I hear the politicians talk about family values a lot; well I am single with no kids. I hear them talk about mortgages and house payments, well I do not have a house nor will I ever be able to even afford one with the garbage paying jobs out there. I just do not feel that myself along with many others in this country are really being paid attention to and like a neglected animal I am now feral and with rabies.

What will it take? Who can do it? Will we even care by that time anyway if someone does come along who is worthy or will we still just rip them apart and go back to the status quo of ignorance, pain, and suffering? I do not know and am not trying to say that I do, however I think there needs to be more like myself writing books, and talking out about how this is not the land of the free anymore and that this is an existence in this country for most, not the pursuit of happiness. I mean I am not going to go into all the statistics and try to claim I am some professor from some esteemed university, but I feel the common person's story is very similar to what is happening to me and the lack of hope and the loss of optimism that I have experienced. I want us as a country to say no more! To again take pride not only in our country but ourselves again. I know that taking pride in myself is also something that has been lost for me and is also over for probably many in congress who are just trying to run the clock out so that they can win and then leave.

It is extremely hard for me and I am sure many Americans to take pride in themselves when they are all broke, having broken marriages, losing jobs, pensions, and being relegated to third class citizens. Our government needs to be checked especially now and in a major way. We need a new party and as the two lords of congress will be tough to fight we can do it we must. I mean just look at what Obama has been able to accomplish with his ground swell of grassroots support. He might not win but even if he does I feel he won't be able to do much or accomplish much different ideas than the republicans. A party that doesn't have a leader who has been in office even once, a party who can take it back, that would be a dream of mine, but as a dreamer I have learned the hard way that very seldom do they come true. And to those critics that say do they have the experience? My rebuttal to that would be that I don't think our founding fathers waited around and joined a party for twenty years before they got started they just saw injustice and made change for the people. President Washington left after two terms because he didn't want another kingdom again unlike our leaders today who will lie, cheat, and steal to stay in power boy how the quality of our leaders today gone down the toilet. That feels good to say however I do no think many will listen nor do I think many care anymore in our country, and I am beginning to be one of them which I hope I can avoid.

CHAPTER SIX

With another week passing here in Milwaukee it is starting to really show the time of change among the colors of the leaves here. The election of 2008 coming around in a few weeks and my birthday in a month which is going to make me 30. I enjoy the fall time of the year as the crispness of the air and the ending of the summer bring about a sort of happiness in me. Maybe because lately I have been pretty beat down by many things occurring in my life and in some way like rain coming down the cold dreary weather mirrors my feelings inside. I recently let my landlady know that after the initial three month lease that I signed with her that I would like to continue to stay here but on a month by month basis. She was more than willing to accommodate this request as I am sure she would have a tough time getting a reliable rent payer that didn't sell drugs or trash the place in here if I were to leave.

I had some conflicting feelings with this decision that I made but I really was totally aimless in any direction and felt that when in total and absolute doubt and with no ambition to move it was wise to just stay put. I wanted to do a bit of fall cleaning like spring cleaning and felt that with this decision maybe something could happen and wanted to illustrate that by making my place clean and giving the aura of a new start here. The place as I described earlier is not that big of a living area so the cleaning really didn't take me all that long to accomplish. The empty beer cans and cigarette butts were the biggest obstacle to my end and besides that a few dishes and trash to remove was all there was. I started to think to myself as I was cleaning that indeed I didn't have much in here besides some beer cans and cigarette butts and it really started to hit me that I was occupying much of my time with this. Of course I didn't have a job or anything else to do so quite rationally I came to the conclusion of so what.

With the apartment looking like it did when I moved in and to my approval I said what the hell go and get more beers to pollute the place with. I mean the bit of optimism or hope that passes through and by me amazes me and it really doesn't last long. I guess I started to feel even more alone in my place now that it was clean how funny that is. I suppose it was like one of those experiences many of us have had of when a roommate moves out and you realize that a lot of the items in the apartment were not yours and thus it leaves a very clear empty spot. I guess then I removed the beer cans and cigarette butts out of the area along with the rest of the filth in some sick way I felt my roommate had moved out as well. Standing there in my boxer shorts and coming to the conclusion of total and utter boredom that was like a cloud ready to dump inches of rain on me I got dressed and headed to the local liquor store on 7th street.

The weather was pretty cold at this time and with the purple clouds hovering overhead and the wind blowing the few remaining leaves off the trees I buttoned up my coat and made way. As I walked through this neighborhood as I have done many times I noticed something quite odd that I never experienced before. It was almost like a ghost town I didn't see anyone around not even the crack heads or bums trying to collect a few cans. I then came to the conclusion that most of the blacks in the area probably do not like the cold weather and maybe this was the reason for the odd atmosphere. To be honest I actually loved the fact that I could walk on my block without feeling to apprehensive. Still besides the absence of the walking dead the area still was a total shit hole and so that let me know I wasn't dreaming.

Walking into the liquor store I go to the back to get my four packs of sixteen ounce beer cans and notice something on the price tag that pisses me off. They raised the damned price! Now I know a quarter extra might not seem like a lot to many of you but it adds up when purchasing four of them every day or every other day you know. I go up with my arms full with the cans and set them down with a look of rage on my face to the attendant. I ask her why they have raised the prices on the beers. She just shrugged her shoulders didn't vocalize a response and rang me up. I got the bubble over my head and thought that they probably raised the prices on these things because I moved into town three months ago and was wiping them out, of course that might not have been the case however that's what I thought to be was the reason. I really hate this liquor store too and all the people that work and hang around this dump. None of them seem to be remotely personable and always have to give you the cold hard stare down that pisses me off royal.

Oh well off I go back to my place as I have repeated it many times and as I do it is starting to get darker. When I open the front gate of the place and walk by Bobby's front porch I notice him lying there on the floor! I was totally shocked and scared and called his name out and no response was met. I again called out and this time I could hear a bit of a moan and see a little body movement. Instantly I dropped my bags crashing them to the concrete below me and rush up the stairs to see what is happening here. I said, "Bobby what the hell is wrong?", and I could tell by the smell and his slurred speech he was knocked out stone cold drunk. I said, "Bobby we have to get you inside it is going to get close to freezing tonight". I said, "Bobby get up man can you get into the house okay?" Bobby then seemed to make an effort at trying to gain his footing but I could clearly see that was not going to happen here today. So I grabbed him and said, "Okay Bobby you have to help me out a bit here". Then I remembered that

Bobby had that bum leg that crippled him when he was younger and I was really only having one leg of his to assist me and not even at half capacity.

So I grabbed and picked him up with all my might and managed somehow to get the front door open which I was surprised it was since he always keeps everything on lockdown. With the door opening I started to wonder whether he was beaten or that someone was in there with him or still might be right now. I didn't really care and managed to carry him to his bed and place him on his back. I looked around carefully and also searched our shared bathroom area and my place too as I thought maybe something might have happened while I was away at the store. With my curiosity and fear aside as I noticed no one was here and that my place was intact. I went back outside to grab my beers and lock his door when I came back in. I went up to him and said, "Bobby what the hell happened man?" He just said that he went and slammed some with his partners that he hangs out with on some north side street somewhere.

I said, "Bobby you didn't do any drugs too did you?", because he was in a state that I almost was for certain that he took something along with the alcohol. But he said no and basically let me know that he just drank or as he puts it, drunk, a lot of whiskey that whole day and was just tired. My god I thought to myself as I imagined the many times I have been totally wrecked probably close to or just as bad as him. I stood there with a beer in my hand and the rest of the cans spread all over his nice hard wood floor and just looked at him. The one light he has lit had the lamp off it to gain better lighting and thus was showing the single bulb. The noise from my room and the television that I left on created a weird atmosphere to say the least. I said, "Bobby you need to lay on your side so if you puke it will not choke to death". With no real response I set my beer down and grabbed a few pillows to prop up his head and upper back so I could adjust him to the proper position.

Once I did that I went back into my kitchen and placed the remaining beers in the fridge. I opened my pack of smokes and took a huge pull off of it as well as the beer I was drinking because lord knows I needed it. I just stood there almost paralyzed and felt terribly sorry for this man. I also came to the thinking that I was glad that I went out that night walking to the store instead of driving somewhere to get them because if I were to have driven there is no way I would have found him. The weather also lately was getting to the low forty's out at night and I started to think that if I hadn't grabbed and pulled him inside that he might have died from hypothermia out there. I was feeling that maybe a higher being had led me to him this night. I am not a very seriously religious man but I just felt that I was in the right place at the right time for him.

After I pounded a few beers and collected myself a bit better I went back in to check on him and also to see if there was anything I could get him before I headed back to my place. Bobby said, "Get my puke bucket". Now the previous times that I have hung out with him he mentioned how he keeps his so-called puke bucket alongside his bed at night in case of he has to vomit. I go, "Bobby are you going to puke right now?", and he replies, "No just get it man". Man this evening is turning into something very heavy to say the least and as I grab the bucket the smell of puke and piss hits me in my face and for a second there I almost needed the bucket for myself. With the bucket placed by his head on the floor I let him know that I am not going to lock his door that leads to the common hall that we share to get to the bathroom and that I will check up on him in awhile.

I didn't have anything to do that evening besides get myself drunk so I figured I could do this every fifteen minutes or so for a few hours and that would be that. Boy was I mistaken. The first few times I headed in all seemed to be okay with him I made sure that he was breathing and that there was no vomiting occurring so I would head back and continue my ritual if you will. I really started to feel the effects of my drinks and was enjoying my clean place and the music which made time fly past quite nicely until I realized I hadn't check on him for like forty five minutes. I instantly jumped up and ran into his room and was met with the most fowl smell of feces. Bob had shit and pissed himself. This is a clear sign he was in trouble as I made sure he was still breathing and that there wasn't any vomit around his mouth or pillows I then shook him and yelled for him to awaken.

Finally after a few minutes of panic he came to and I said, "Bobby you have to wake up man you shit your self". It took him a few more minutes to actual be aware that something was wrong and he said, "What the fuck is that smell man?"   I quickly let him know that he indeed had soiled himself and that he needed to get out of these clothes and try to clean himself up a bit. Now about an hour and a half has elapsed since I placed him there so he wasn't as drunk as before but was clearly still in la la land. I could tell that I was going to have to assist him with getting his clothes off and into the shower and I really did not want to do this. I could not stand the smell I mean take ten baby diapers and mix it with piss and dirty clothes and put your hands in it then place your hands on your face it was terrible! I frantically looked around for a second option maybe just get a towel and pray he can get out of his clothes and then just place the towel on him or something. Unfortunately I knew deep down inside my soul that wasn't humane or appropriate for this situation.

I tell him that he needs to assist me and get his clothes off and that I will help him into the shower once he gets naked. Bobby was clearly showing that he was embarrassed but me being a drunk to I said, "Fuck it man it happens to us all". With that little bit of encouragement we get him naked and I throw the soiled clothing to the corner of the room and by doing so get a nice helping hand of shit. Now remember how I told you earlier that Bobby had contracted polio as a child and had a gimp leg? Well that gimp leg also had some sort of brace on it that we needed to get off because it could not be in the water. This situation is really challenging my most outer limits to tell you the truth. I finagle with the damned thing and get the sock off this leg and am appalled at the sight of his limb. It is very mal formed and looks almost like some sort of stump structure with toes! This sight made me gasp and take a step back and I was really at this time needing Bobby's puke buck, but I raged on with the task at hand thinking the quicker I get it done the better. So with him butt naked as the day he was born, and with shit in his ass like a baby that needed to be wiped I get him into the tub and crank the water on high. I threw him his washcloth or rag that he had in there and gave him a bar of ivory soap that I used and sat on the toilet watching him bathe.

As the bathing went on we chatted a bit and I grabbed a much needed beer and smoked a cigarette to help not only with my nicotine craving but also with the horrendous stench that was coming off him. The water started to turn brown and with every swipe of his rag he was starting to feel cleaner again I could see it in his face. I could see that he was in some way totally unaware as to what happened and also looking embarrassed cleaning off in front of another man. We finally could see that he was clean after removing the water a few times and starting over and so I went into his place and grabbed his robe off one of the hangers he hangs his clothes on. When I was doing this I began to thinking of the first few times I hung out with him and being impressed at the cleanliness of his place. The condition that he was in this evening was in direct contrast to this and I became a bit worried for his future even more and hoping that this would not be repeated again.

I rushed back and give him his robe and with a look of thanks upon his face he yells, "Okay playa get me to bed and thanks man I owe you one". I just nodded with a smile and put his arm around my neck and led him into his place back to his bed like a boxer who just suffered the worst beating of his life. After placing him in there and saying that I am glad I could help I left his door still a bit open and returned back to my place to clean up with the most industrial cleaning products I had around. I had bleach thank god and plenty of it and I also removed my clothing to because I was soiled now by this time. I made it a point to tell him the next day that he was going to thoroughly clean up the mess that was still in that bathroom because I am telling you I wasn't going to shower in there till bleach was poured over everything. Once cleaned up I headed back into my place and sat Indian style on the floor and started to do some reflection and also pat myself on the back for a very humane thing that I just did and thought I lost the capacity for.

Sitting there and digesting what I just witnessed it came to me that I in fact have been at the mercy of my actions and others in the past as well. I needed some nice cool crisp fresh air and went out onto my back porch. With the wind really starting to blow hard and the night sky shimmering a bit with the lights of the city shining on it I felt thankful that night. Thankful that for at least this moment I wasn't in Bobby's place. I think it is hard for me as well as many of us to see the bad in ourselves until we see someone that mirrors what we do. That is at least the emotions that were coming to me; however with the state of my place in this world I didn't seem to care for any real length of time about myself it just passed on by.

The next morning came or rather afternoon and I went to check on Bobby and see how he was managing because I know after one of those bouts it can knock you off your ass for days. The door was still open from the night before as the way I left it so I figured I would find him in bed also. There he was with the TV on in a bad state. I asked him if there was anything that he needed and all he could ask for was water. I told him after he recuperated that I would appreciate it if he would clean up the bathroom and said I could provide the bleach. Bobby didn't say no and again thanked me for my assistance the previous evening. I sat there a bit just talking with him and he was saying that he isn't going to do that again, I swear that should be the drinker motto. I laughed and now knowing he was going to be fine said my goodbye and left because I needed to head downtown and check my P.O box and drop off some dry cleaning in the hopes I might get a job interview soon.

I usually like to drop off my dry cleaning once in awhile because I either wear it when I go out to the one bar on the block trying to look hip and because want to get the smoke smell out of the fabric. Going downtown to where I have my mailbox and do the dry cleaning is always an interesting drive. I see the usual suspects now or at least I am starting to recognize them on the corners waiting for a John or their next hit. The once used playgrounds that have long been neglected and are not in any shape for children to play on. The bombed out looking houses and the businesses that have also left is amazing to me, but once you cross the bridge and enter downtown Milwaukee it's like day and night.

After dropping of my dry cleaning and checking my mailbox only to find nothing in there I remembered that I wanted to check for jobs at the library again and apply for a few if possible. At the library they have a listing of city positions that are open and I thought what the heck I am not getting any luck with the internet and the papers so I checked. Well let's see here I see a job posting for a nuisance control officer one position that I feel I am more than qualified for. What it was in essence was a glorified garbage and filth enforcer with the city. I wouldn't be an actual garbage man, rather go on calls that were made to the city regarding houses, yards, or streets that people in the neighborhood would say are unkempt. The qualifications I met with my degree, and being that my last job in Ann Arbor before I moved here I worked at a bank I figured that would meet there enforcement of rules qualification.

So I went online to the city's website as computers were fortunately open today and printed off the ten pages that I needed to apply for the position. The job posting said college was a requirement so I also printed off a transcript request form from Central Michigan University my alma mater. Once I had all these papers that I needed I sent the transcript request with the appropriate address for them to send it to and then went home to fill out the forms for the city job. Finally, at last, I thought an actually good paying job open and a city one no less. The benefits and all that I am sure would be second to none and once employed I figured this could possibly be a position that would be almost impossible to get fired from. After an hour I would say I had all the information in the blanks to the best of my ability of course because they asked for everything except my blood type. I needed stamps so I got back in my car and headed downtown to send this out right away. It is amazing how your spirits can be lifted at the prospect of applying for a decent job and also thinking that you have a good chance.

I was very proud of myself in a few hours I accomplished a lot. I felt instead of sending resumes online and attaching them which by the way is how it is done I felt I actually did something and was very hopeful for the first time in awhile. Of course after doing something productive I must counter that by doing some counter to that and I decided I earned a few cold ones not like I ever need an excuse for that. So I am off to the mighty pic and save downtown as it was on my way back anyway. Coming back with beer in tow and my thoughts feeling good I soak it in like a sunny day in Alaska after the months of darkness have passed. I enjoy the feeling of I doing something good today that might help me and gain me some good employment. I tell you when you are in a pretty dark place like I have been you grab onto any sign of hope you can. The only problem with that is that you don't want to get your hopes up too much because if that doesn't come through it can be devastating.

The day today shall be a good one I say to myself and I will not let anyone or anything ruin it. This day is good I am going to enjoy my beer and smokes and I have some good pasta that I will cook up with the mushroom alfredo that I am addicted to later after I tie a good one on. The history channel has some show about aliens which I love and I think hey man enjoy the good atmosphere while you can because it can be gone in a flash.

I don't know how many of you all believe in the concept of life on other planets, but I think it is more than likely that there is. I often think how the world would react if it was actually confirmed and people knew for a fact that indeed we are not alone. More than likely I assume it would result in total and utter anarchy. I guess in some way I don't think it is a bad thing that I am a bit of a nerd because I enjoy the bizarre theories and also the bizarre people that propose them.

Anyway the day is going off well I have all that I need and these last few days not only do I feel I have saved someone's life but I also applied for a city job so that isn't a bad week. With the almost manic feeling rushing threw me I decided to call my mother and father to let them know about the job as I haven't had any joy or good news to send their way in awhile. They seemed happy for me but I also heard a sense of reservation on them as to being worried that I already had gotten my hopes up too much. Nevertheless, good news would be sent out to the cosmos and when you have good news especially in my desert of apathy you really need to yell it out.

CHAPTER SEVEN

The next week was election time and I of course was an Obama supporter and was hopeful for him but worried for another stolen election in some way. The whole process of running for president to me was ridiculous. I mean they start running like two years in advance making it a total political garbage overload. There should be some rule that dictates the time when you can announce and start running so that the American people are not subject to all the phone calls and commercials. And of course these liars always try to promise the same shit every four years and every four years nothing gets accomplished. That is why as I stated earlier that I feel we need a third or even fourth party in this country to actual shake things up. The American political process is to me like a stagnant pond, the water isn't worth drinking.

As usual I stay and watch the night of most elections as I am concerned as to what person will be guiding our country in the next few years. However I cannot escape the fact that I am just killing time and am not going to see anything that much different than what we had before. I am sure there are many out there that feel the exact same way I do and are at the verge of just throwing their hands up in defeat. As the night progresses the states are being called and for the most part there are no surprises as usual. And then some of the usual red states go Obama and I start to think he is actually going to win, and win he did! I think that maybe we will have someone different and with energy and vision to move us forward. I see in this man a great talent that we as a nation should be proud of. Though there is a saying that once someone meets there role model or idol they are often less than impressed, I just hope that doesn't come true here with Obama's election.

The next morning I grab the paper and see the headlines and for an instant there it was like was I dreaming last night? Is this real? I called a few friends to discuss if the country is not going to be over and if he can salvage this mess. One of my friends was pretty adamant that nothing was really going to change that it would all be the same old stunts. I asked him why he thought that considering having the first black president was a sign hopefully that we as a country were going to be more progressive. He laughed with great amusement and with sarcasm basically stated that he's going to be a mediocre president at best and that the old white man establishment isn't going to work with him. Now I shot back at this and said like black on black crime the old white guys have been fighting each other for power since the beginning of the republic and to make it a racial issue is a bit unfortunate.

That racial comment by my friend really started to work its way in me like a sliver you just cannot manage to get out of your hand. I am so sick and god damn tired of all the racial bullshit that we as a country talk about. It is 2008 and granted there might need to be more progress but shit there is going to be a black president now. I as a white male am tired of those types of comments my friend made implying that only white people can be racist and backwards. I have had many encounters here in Milwaukee that would put that statement in serious jeopardy. I don't know I think people that are so superficial like that need to live around others that are different than themselves in order to make an even basic assumption on a group of people.

Anyway I do not want to go into that anymore right now as it really burns my ass. I called a different friend and he was ecstatic about the election and thought that things indeed were going to change. I asked him like my other friend why he came to that conclusion. He in essence said that now it is our generation that is going to determine the outcome of our country. He admitted that first the older generation must die off, which I was like amen to, but once that happens hopefully we will be more understanding and compassionate as a country to each other those words rang true for me. The good old boys say just pull yourselves up by your bootstraps and get it done yourselves, but things like that just isn't happening anymore today. I like when Obama mentioned this and said that what if you have no boots to begin with? Yes, yes, yes preach on brother and I think we as a country are starting to see that those who have the benefits of money and access can say those things, but to be truly in a disadvantaged place and make it without some help is virtually impossible.

I wanted to recapture the feeling of feeling good that I had a week or so ago when I applied to that city of Milwaukee position but was having cautious optimism. I have pretty much lost all optimism for my life and that of this country through this last several months and it angers me when a president with such possibilities gets elected that I am skeptical. Again that is what is so wrong with our country we are so used to having less than competent officials represent us that we are like a beaten child around a new stepfather, worried and cautious. We have to get our backbones and some courage and demand better representation form our elected officials. I wish honestly we could go up to the hill in Washington and just have a politician toss wouldn't that be great.

As the days went by I thought less and less about the election and worried more about me and my immediate situation. I still hadn't heard anything from the city and now it has been three or maybe now four weeks later and I am starting to feel that my hope was for not. I still saw Bobby now and again and we usually would get together and slam some beers in my room while watching Unsolved Mysteries reruns. He seemed pretty worse off like me lately and even with the election he too was temporarily enthused but then like myself was more like well I need to worry about me right now. He was having a tough time getting some social security disability money worked out as that is what he has lived on because he is a cripple. I could understand being at the mercy of a handout for your livelihood because I too was on assistance with my unemployment insurance.

He didn't have a car and had to take the bus everywhere and now that it was coming to the end of November it was getting really cold and waiting for a bus line wasn't that fun. I offered many times to take him to wherever it was that he needed to go to but he would never accept that. I asked him if Obama would make it easier for him now that he was going to be in office in a few months in January. Bobby was like maybe but probably not. I guess in some way it is a bit of a stretch of the imagination to expect one person to solve all our problems right people. I mean like I have mentioned before we have like five hundred other idiots messing everything up here too. I had my routine in some way like all of us I was trying to get things done applying to jobs when applicable and worthy, but besides that I mainly was held up drinking beer and watching TV in my place all day long.

Well my thirty year old birthday was coming up and that was a very unwanted milestone for me especially at this time in my life. I thought when I was eighteen that I was going to be somebody and actually achieve something, what a crock that was. No in fact at eighteen even though I already had perfected a nice rage portfolio I was very optimistic regarding my future. You know go to college major in business be a mover and a shaker all that crap. Meet some trophy wife with great assets and probably pop out Johnny and Janey and live in some suburb somewhere. It is funny I thought back then that it was the life I wanted to possess now that I am older and with a shit load more experience am laughing at those that do that or perhaps I am jealous on a sub conscience level. Yeah most of the people I talk to regarding this that are older being as I always have held friendships with those that were a few years ahead of me say that I am still young and do not need to be discouraged.

Now that advice in most cases when it is looked at comes from people who are doing okay and are for the most part happy where they are in life or at least that is the image they are showing me. Also since the election of Obama I see in him this ambition and intelligence that I truly do not see in myself and in a way I hate him for that at times. Weird I know but I am a total mystery even to myself many of the times. I guess a lot of it is and I think I have heard this saying before is that you cannot judge yourself by comparing yourself to others. I so wish that we as humans could do this saying, however I think in this society where we are told to buy and consume and have the car and house and all that crap that envy is alive and well here. I don't know I wish I could take a happy pill and be in la la land, oh wait there are pills that can do that I forgot. Thirty fricken years old, huh, what to do with my thirty's that was different than the total disaster that my twenties turned out to be.

I heard on the radio the other day about how this college was saying if you have your bachelors and things are rough why not go back and get your masters degree. I wanted to vomit. I mean c'mon now college is a racket unless you go to the right one and have all the right connections that will basically give you a job. I mean please society stop trying to sell this almost thirty year old broke douche bag anything because I do not have the damn money okay! So what am I going to do now that the thirties are upon me? I could always travel the country like a hippie hobo cat I suppose but that sounds awful to me. I am already continuing to search for god awful paying jobs with no future so I am doing that so check that off. Oh well my mind is blanker than Bush's head right now. I don't know I just thought by now I would have acquired at least a home of my own instead of living in these rooms paying ridiculous rent to these slum lords. I know that my story is not unique and all that but I am not saying much to my friends and family about these things I just mentioned because if

I get a comment that says, "shut up man you think you are the only one?", I probably would beat the hell out of them. That is right people shut up and be quiet be seen not heard.

The day here is November 24 and I am now thirty years old. The cards have come or a few less than the previous years but are very appreciated. The typical phone call from the parents wishing me well which is nice, but it is hard trying to sound up beat when you are not. For my birthday I really didn't do anything different than what I have been doing for the last year which is just going and grabbing a few cold ones and hanging out. Now normally I would have ordered myself a pizza and wings which is usually what I do, however since I live in the hood there are absolutely no places that deliver to this shit hole. I figured it isn't good to be alone on your birthday so I hollered at Bobby to come on down like the price is right and slam a few with me. Bobby is always accommodating especially if I am providing the refreshments. I told him it was my birthday and he said happy one man, and said now lets watch some TV. I have to tell you it was nice to have him over because it stopped me from being negative for a bit which is exactly what I needed to do on this day. You know sit back have a few and talk with a friend about what your watching so I was happy he kept me company that day.

I have always been impressed with those that are very determined and that set certain goals that by a certain age they will have accomplished either a marriage, job, car, or what have you. The determination I have witnessed by the few I have encountered who are staying straight forward on the path to success, or at least what I believe success is from what society has taught me. I guess for myself I have always been floating along waiting for something or someone to really light my fire, and always seem to not attain that. Maybe it is because since a child I never really felt adequate and to be an important person. These feelings as I have touched on earlier have been with me my entire life and I really do not know why. Perhaps it was my upbringing which I never really felt was a very nurturing or loving one rather to stay out of our way type of vibe at least that is what I always felt. I am not bashing my parents or anything I am sure they did the best they could its just I think maybe that hurt my self determination a bit.

What is funny about that statement is that my brother is very successful and was from day one very goal oriented and seemed to be on a mission going somewhere positive. So maybe it is my laziness and lack of self discipline I do not know. I have talked to a few people over the years about just this. Many say that you need to be passionate about something and go for it. To be quite honest people I really haven't been turned on by anything really. I mean I usually start something that is an obvious reach for me perhaps writing this book and I seem to always fall terribly short. To be thirty years old and basically be almost as vulnerable as a child and be also unable to barely support myself on the garbage jobs out there really makes really reinforces my feeling inadequate. Maybe like the saying goes I shouldn't compare myself to others to find my personal value. Maybe I should start comparing myself to the bums on the street or someone in a third world country maybe then I would look at myself in a more positive light. The pressure that society puts on especially men to be the provider and all that really is something I believe in. I have a few friends that are now married and with children and are barely making it. I do not want to be in that position ever or put a child of mine through poverty or struggle. We didn't have much either initially in my upbringing and to be honest I didn't care, but for me personally it would destroy my feeling of being a man if I had to be in that position for any real length of time. My father did provide very well as the years went by and he worked like a dog and made sure we had a roof over our heads and food in my stomach, and to this day holds the same job he has had now for thirty years. I am amazed by this because now a day's jobs last barely three years.

I just feel like I don't know if I could or want to work one job either though for thirty years. I am a dreamer I guess or I don't know what to classify myself as but I just want to be moved I want to feel life and I feel that the work till you drop mentality that our society has put us into like drones is frightening as hell to me. You know how you hear people saying that it is about assimilating into the group think or being apart of the group that no one person is very special. Dammit I want to be me and not be as unidentifiable as the next person in the cubicle next to me; this just really perplexes me at this time of my life. I guess at thirty that is why I don't have what I in some sick way crave yet also despise. I am not a good shut the hell up and keep your head down type of a person.

I was talking to a friend of mine who is knocking on forty hear shortly about just this subject of where are we going to be and what do we want out of life? He was terribly cynical and said I was making the same shit money you were at thirty but I am still making the shit money at forty. Not only that he went into saying that his marriage is failing and he is now with a child in the relationship and is too terrified about the provider role and all that comes with that. He was like I want to move out of this country as he said the social contract here is broken. He didn't feel like the stressing of material possessions and having huge houses that one cannot afford was a model for him, as well as he stated he could not even come close to achieving it leaving him with feelings of inadequacy that I am now feeling as well. I was amazed and comforted by his words and frustrations because I find that when I talk about things that matter in life like this to the majority of men especially those being good little drones I get a regurgitated almost script like bullshit response from those types.

Well I am now thirty something and I need to somehow find a good mix for me and only me. I mean I in a lot of ways as I am sure you can tell I have thought about these issues plenty. To me what would be a bit of bliss is not having to pay rent to some slum lord so he can pay his mortgage off. I would love to have my own house in the next few years; nothing to significant just something that would be mine. I don't need five thousand square feet three bedrooms two baths and a two door garage. Just somewhere and something to call my own and feel good about it. As far as women go I think I would like one however marriage is a huge stretch for me personally. I don't think I can find an American woman who isn't turned on by money and possessions. I guess what it really comes down to is that I need to be me no matter how old I get and if that means that I am alone the rest of my life then so be it I guess.

I know this might sound a bit hypocritical or judgmental but I think we all need to really at some point in our lives reflect on where we are, where we want to go, and also what is really going to make us happy. I know that this sounds a bit cheesy perhaps but I wish we all would realize that the human spirit is being killed by this machine of society and greed. To be a good worker bee and work till you drop. For us not to question anything after a certain age because shit you cannot do anything about it anyway. I just didn't think that you stopped learning or having the ability to re-evaluate your situation after a certain age. To me I find that most people are already dead but just don't know it. I also when in conversation with many people find myself terribly bored and un stimulated by their words. Who knows right maybe I will just start my own commune, wouldn't that be great.

CHAPTER EIGHT

Where is the response from the City of Milwaukee concerning that job I applied to came into my head this morning as I didn't see anything in the mail today. I applied to the job quite a while ago and am starting to think it was a huge waste of my time and hope. Over the last few weeks of course I have been trying to get gainful employment but man I am telling you there isn't anything around. I mean I even applied for a call center job at a department store basically for ten dollars an hour doing customer service calls. I checked my email the other day at the library and found that I received a rejection email that said my qualifications do not meet their current requirements: I was sick to my stomach with rage. What the hell is going on in this so called greatest country? I suppose I shouldn't sound too angry or even surprised by this outcome as I have been getting told no thank you so much I should be numb to it by now.

The other day right after I got this message in my email I was watching television and my TV of like fourteen years took a total dump on me and like zapped to black right in the middle of a program I was really into. I thought for a moment that perhaps it was some kind of power outage or surge so I went around the dump to check the other fixtures to see if they were out also. Well much to my pleasant surprise they weren't so I felt that this was great news. So I go back and turn the TV on again and it brings up the program and I think nothing of it. About ten minutes later the screen goes black except for a line of light in the middle of it and I can still hear the commentary coming from the tube but cannot see the picture. So about this time I am starting to be less dense and know that it is an old TV that I had since high school and with great reluctance know that now my TV is dead.

Let the hits just keep on coming on man. Now to me the TV is basically my only sense of entertainment besides getting bombed and going to the bar once in awhile and I know that I do not have nearly the cash to buy a new TV so what the hell am I going to do about this I say as I stand with my hands on my hips naked in the room. The rage mounting, the can't anything be easy for me cram my already tight head and I just scream at the top of my lungs, "fuuuuck!" Bobby next door must have heard my cry of agony and knocks on my door asking what's going on. I open the door with only my boxer shorts on now as I had to put something on and look at him and say nothing works for me nothing. I tell him that my long lost friend of my TV has passed away and I am screwed now. Bobby a bit unhappy too I could tell as he would often come over to my place and watch TV with me because his TV is totally ghetto and all the colors are messed up.

What are you going to do he asks me. I replied with a half crazed look I am assuming and said jump off a bridge. With that somehow that broke the tension and he started to laugh his ass off and puts his hand on my should and goes Lee you crazy man. I too had to laugh I mean this is getting so damn ridiculous as to how bad shit is going it almost doesn't surprise me that the hits just keep on keeping on. Bobby said come over to my place lets have a few cold ones. Now that is my man, he knows that's what I need right now and also that I needed some company and I gladly with total glee and like a fairy hopped over to his place. I tell you shit has got to get better here because I am starting to see the rope fray and I don't know how long it will hold me.

When I get into Bobby's I laugh inside as his TV which by the was is a total piece of shit is playing Bonanza of all things. I started in by asking him whether he liked the show or it was just a mis input on this remote. He goes hell yeah man I love Bonanza it's a great show. Now picture this a black man with a gimpy leg and wool hat on who listens to hip hop and r&b all the time and lives in the hood of Milwaukee and is totally proud of being black watching Bonanza? I nearly was pissing myself laughing at the total disconnect I was experiencing at the time here. Man did I need that laugh and also the cold one that he slapped loosely at me. We sat there me in my boxers him with his usual flannel attire on and watched Bonanza at I believe ten in the morning. Bobby then said man aren't you freezing your ass off right now? I go yeah I am it has been getting pretty cold in this dank ass house lately hasn't it. Bobby goes damn straight I don't think the heat is even working in this place as I haven't heard it turn on once.

When I go back into my room to put on some clothes I start to think about that and yes too noticed that it has been unusually cold in the place and that I haven't felt any heat kick on either. Now it is December now and is totally freezing outside so we should be having the heat come on a regular basis I would think. Bobby was right the heat isn't working at all and to be quite honest I am unsure as to why I am surprised by this to tell you the truth. So I grab a few beers and smokes and head back into Bobby's to watch some Bonanza. When I get back in I see that Bobby has opened up his stove and left the door open and I ask him why. He said that at least it is some heat coming in the place. Man alive I thought what a shithole we live in nothing ever works I swear. Bobby started to swear about it too and say that we needed to call our landlady and complain. Then I thought that she would more than likely blow us off and make my rage even worse so I said to him that maybe we should wait a bit longer to make sure it is not working so we have good grounds to complain.

Now Bobby especially can be very irritable at times, which I find comforting because if you were happy living in this situation

I would have to seriously question ones sanity. Here we are both bundled up with three or so layers of clothing on drinking beers, watching Bonanza and having an oven as our heat source no truer of a picture could be painted here. Eventually as the hour progressed Bobby started ranting about the situation he was in and how bad it sucked. He was clearly a man in distress and I liken it only to the type of madness one would probably attain being in solitary confinement for years at a prison somewhere. I sat there just listening and nodding my head back and forth as to reaffirm my disgust as well and let him vent it out.

I then went back into my place to grab more beers and noticed I was on fumes and asked Bobby if he wanted to go downtown with me to grab some more if for nothing else to get out of this dump for a bit. Bobby seemed more than willing to accompany me and also I think too he needed more beers and knew that I would be able to supply him with more if he came with me. As we were leaving a man that lived a block away from us was trying to hit us up for some cash, and this pissed Bobby off something fierce. Bobby was like get the hell out of here how dare you come into our parking lot unannounced. I was a bit taken aback by his rage, but remembered that today just wasn't a good day to be messing with a poor broke down man like him. The man went off and I was a bit embarrassed but also felt that he was right in acting that way because for the few months now that I have been here I have been hit up many times too and it drives me nuts.

The drive was interesting as well as Bobby just sort of sat there looking out the window being very quiet. Bobby I said to him what's the matter man? He just said all this bullshit as he pointed out the window at the bums and broken down houses we passed along the way. I was glad to have him being honest with me and letting me see the true side of him I felt it was a sign that he and I were becoming friends. Once we get to the store I figured I would have to get about twenty four beers and a pack of smokes for us to hold us over. Every time I actually bought like Budweiser or a name brand unlike the sixteen ounce ice beer four packs Bobby would be like we gonna be drinking well tonight huh. It was humbling to hear him say things like that because to many those beers would still be sub par but to Bobby it was like drinking champagne. I have to tell you that it was nice to be around another person who wasn't fake for once. He was just as broken and flawed as me maybe worse and didn't seem to want to hide it anymore. Most people just give you lip service bullshit all the time and are unwilling or incapable of letting you know how things are really going for them, but with Bobby and me we were like why try faking anything anymore.

When we returned he was in a better mood I think in part because he just needed to vent and also having more beers always cheered him up for at least a while anyway. As we entered into my place he noticed I think for the first time my paintings that I had propped on the floor near the wall beside my kitchen table. He said you paint? I go I used to. He seemed interested in them and asked to look them over I of course didn't object. Man these aren't half bad man he states, and I being a person who craves compliments was very encouraged by his words. Why don't you paint anymore he asked me. I stood there with the case of beers in my hand and with the snow on my shoes melting on the floor beneath me I simply said, "no one thinks I am worthy enough to be displayed." Shit he goes those cats don't know anything. To be honest I was thinking yeah they do because I think they are pretty shitty myself.

I don't know if he was giving me serious lip service because I was supplying him with beverages, but I didn't think he was lame enough to be that calculating. I told him how when I was back in Ann Arbor I tried to get some of my work displayed at the art center there in town and that I met up with this prissy white snob bitch who didn't seem to want to take interest in my work. He was like yeah I bet that must have driven you nuts huh. Well it did I guess like I said before I was searching for some talent I might posses and thought that maybe I had some and that it might be able to be seen by other people and appreciated by them as well. The lady was very snobby and finally agreed to put one of my paintings up in the store gallery part of the center and try to sell it. With that I was pretty optimistic thinking wouldn't it be a trip to see my work hanging up somewhere with a price tag on it. One of my friends at the time was going to go to the art fair that is annually held here in Ann Arbor and wanted to stop by the center and look at my work. So one day he calls me up and said that he didn't see my painting hanging up anywhere in the center. I was shocked and now totally embarrassed because he was down there with another one of our friends telling her its here and to have it not there was a huge disappointment. Bobby was like man I would have gone down there and cussed that bitch out. I laughed and told him I did just that. Screw this he then said lets go grab some beers and try to forget about the many disappointments we have had, okay man. With no reluctance and feeling good about venting myself a bit we went back to watching old school westerns, drinking beer and huddling near the open oven.

The next day I was hoping to hear back from the City of Milwaukee regarding the job I applied to a few months back. Since I came here in August I haven't had one single interview, no scratch that I had a possible interview with this leasing corporation that called me for one back in October. I believe they dealt in leasing major machinery equipment for businesses as I can remember. The job was at a downtown location and I figured that they would probably have good offices thus leading me to conclude that the opportunities might not be half bad. Now the job posting that I saw in the paper when I applied to this job was listing a hourly rate of around thirteen an hour which is crap but considering I was pretty desperate I applied anyway. I received a phone call from my landlady the day I was notified about the job interview that was to happen in two days. She wanted to come over with some window guy to try to see if we needed new windows for the winter. I of course filled with hope told her I had an interview with a company downtown in a few days. I really don't know why I told her this however I feel it was in some way trying to illustrate to her that I wasn't a bum and also perhaps to ease her mind that I would be able to continue paying my rent in the long term.

The day of my interview came and I just got finished cleaning up in the bathroom and was on my way to looking very fresh and clean. When I was in my room I could hear her opening the doors and walking up the stairs that were just outside my place. I put on my pants and opened the door that led to the hallway that had our bathroom and saw her. She said are you ready for your interview today? I was like ready as I'll ever be I guess. Bobby must have heard the commotion going on and flung his door open looking a bit agitated at the sight of all these people just feet from his door. Our landlady said, "oh Bobby I tried to call you and let you know I was stopping by today but your machine messages were all full and you never answered your phone the previous times that I called." Bobby was still not to open to dialogue and said, "do you need to come in?", and our landlady said, "no we are just checking some windows around the house." After all that I proceeded to get ready as my interview was around two hours away at this point.

I was starting to come together like a well oiled machine and felt that this job was mine for the taking. I also grabbed my cell phone to turn that on to see if I had any messages form the previous evening. Mainly the messages I had however were from damn collectors wanting to get water out of this dry well. I heard the bing bing noise on it letting me know I had either a text message or a voice mail message. I went and grabbed it off the kitchen table and saw that I had a voice mail. Now voice mails always make me nervous for some reason at this point in my life because I felt that it would be somebody either wanting to collect money from me or someone wanting to yell at me. With great hesitance I punched in my password to unlock the message and listened. You have one new message the operator voice said to me. The message was from the business that I was to interview with that day. The lady on the phone said that her and her boss had re-evaluated my resume and felt with my qualifications that I was over qualified for the position that they were looking to fill.

I was stunned standing there with most of my nice clothes on and my belt not connected and laying half open on my waist and I had to replay the message. Indeed it was true the message said just what I thought I heard that the interview was cancelled and I wasn't going to have a shot at it because I was over qualified. What the fuck I say aloud and toss my phone down on my half deflated air mattress with rage ready to burst out my ears like a volcano. Fuck I exclaimed with a hearty yell that would definitely be heard by my landlord and other housemates but what did I care. My landlady probably a bit alarmed came down and said, "what happened?", looking frightened and nervous at hearing such rage. I said, "listen to this bullshit", as I went and grabbed my phone and played the ridiculous message for her. As the message played Bobby now came out as well and we all stood there listening to me being told I cannot interview because I am too qualified. My landlady just stood there along with Bobby looking at the ground afterward and then saying, "man that is awful Lee sorry to hear that man."

Another rejection for possible employment I mean I can handle the rejection emails that I have gotten, or the few letters that I have also received in the mail letting me know I do not meet the requirements for a ten dollar an hour job. This however was different because I was two hours away from the damned thing and I was all ready to go. I said thank you to them and said to my landlady, "you see the bullshit one has to go through in this economy." I mean I thought getting an education would open doors for you like so many bastards have preached to me right. Remember in the earlier part of this novel I brought this up briefly well this is one of the examples I have. I felt so thrown away by not being able to interview for this position solely because I was over qualified. Now people let me tell you I am not a genius and I don't have super highly skilled intelligence with business at least that's what I think. Yes a college education closes doors for you too especially in this god forsaken economy where they want to have people working for such slave wage pay.

Bobby came on over with a beer in hand and limping on over with a look of understanding said, "man what a bitch bro here have one on me." I grabbed it and sucked it down like it was the antidote for a severe snake bite. We both went into my bedroom part of the place and I sat Indian style down with my black dress pants on and nice shirt half buttoned and exhaled with a huge whoosh. I turned to my left as Bobby always sat in the one chair I had in the room and said, "Bobby what the fuck man what possibilities do I have if I am being told I am over qualified for a thirteen dollar an hour job man." Bobby being as nice as possible was telling me not to give this any real importance and to basically say screw it. I mean did it really take these idiots at this business two days to figure that I was over qualified for their more than likely monkey job. And to cancel two hours before the interview really chapped my white ass. The nerve of employers today was tattooed even more so on my psyche with this development.

So me and Bobby sat and drank and just stayed silent a bit looking at the TV that wasn't on thinking. I decided I needed another beer and a smoke and also that music might be able to calm this beast down a notch so I turned on the XM radio we get through our cable plan. I threw off the clothes that I had been wearing for this interview and tossed them on the ground. Forget the fact that the week before I paid like twenty dollars to dry clean this one outfit. Twenty dollars that I should have spent on food or drink rather than even imagine that I might have a slight chance at some shitty paying job. Man life is putting me to the test lately and I am failing with flying colors. I like to tell myself that it isn't me that is failing, but the economy which I am in and to be honest I actually believe that even with all my self pity and hatred I know I am trying hard here to still succeed in some way. As I said earlier in the book, "oh how does it suck not being anybody, and not having a way to change some things."

Total apathy replaces total rage and me and Bobby just sat there both in utter and total defeat.

I had another interview as well one at a car dealership a bit before that last fiasco. This was an interesting interview it was supposed to be working with some financing company that helped customers get financing so they could purchase a car through the dealership. I of course was terribly skeptical because the economy was taking a big dump and everyday all I saw on the news was how credit is drying up. Nevertheless, I thought what the hell I needed work and thought that I could do this job well as my last job in Ann Arbor gave me some experience with finance. I laid off the booze for a few days to let myself feel and look better as I had a three day window before the interview was to take place. That morning of the interview I got up and felt like I needed to seriously talk myself up as I wasn't to confident about my interview skills because it was a year since I had one.

Going into the bathroom to shave I looked into the mirror and thought what a sexy bitch I am. Talking myself up was essential but also going to take more than that I can remember saying to myself. With the shaving cream applied I starting shaving of a weeks worth of facial hair like I was mowing a lawn strip by strip. As the shaving progressed I could hear that Bobby was listening to some nice old school type r&b music which was a nice contribution to my grooming activity. I hate shaving and never have liked it that's probably why I only shave when absolutely necessary. I thought back to the time when I was a teenager and getting my first facial hair for some reason that morning. I can remember thinking about how odd it was as now I am a man and thinking about this time in my life for some reason. I remember how I was so proud to get those first few hairs on my chinny chin chin right, and of course those almost dirt looking ones that come on your upper lip.

Anyway getting back to the story at hand I was finished with all the grooming and was getting dressed. The car dealership was quite a few miles from where I lived here in the hood and I was anxious about finding it the first time and not getting lost. Of course I map quested it the previous day and pretty sure that getting lost would not be an issue, but I still was a bit shaky on it. I walked out the door and immediately felt uneasy because I looked very nice among the filth that surrounded me. I remember thinking get to your car and leave as fast as you can you don't want anyone in the hood seeing you all dressed up like that because then they might think you have money. And in the hood if these desperate bastards think there is money somewhere they just might want to come grab it while I am gone.

I managed to get into the car and escape quickly into civilization and found the dealership perfectly with fifteen minutes to spare I believe. I walked into the dealership and was asked if I could be helped with anything. Yeah now I know I looked nice and probably like I had my shit together but I was thinking yeah help me out with a job man. I also remember thinking that I would never ever be able for at least the near future be able to purchase my own car. And also how nice it must be to actually purchase a new car for yourself, as I wouldn't know because the only care I have ever known was generously given to me by my brother. Well with the man asking me if I could be helped I said yes that I was here for an interview with so and so I cannot remember the douche bags name right now. I waited in the lobby for this man and on the TV the guys had some soft porn looking show on with women baring almost it all. No they weren't naked or having sex but they were all in bikinis and really trying to show off their assets pardon the pun. This show went on for another fifteen minutes and I started to feel a bit uncomfortable for the women walking around this place I mean blatant sexual harassment could have been proved I here I believe.

"Lee, Lee Sanford", a gentleman said to my right, I go that's me. So the man came in that was to interview me interrupting my soft core pervert viewing. The interview started with the basics so what brought you to Milwaukee and all that. I said that I needed a change from Ann Arbor and was hoping for a new fresh start here. I said a bigger city might be able to offer more jobs you know garbage like that. Then he started to get into more of the questions and asked why I applied for this job. Oh brother he did not go there did he. I absolutely hate this question it is probably by far the most annoying question beside where do you picture yourself in five years. I wanted to scream at him that I am unemployed and need a job and that is about it. Or should I say well Mr. Useless I have been dreaming about working in a car dealership since I was five years old. I cannot think of a better opportunity or job than this, this would be my dream come true right?

To make this agony go by fast the interview lasted just about a half hour and we talked about the job and my past positions I have had and he said he would call me no matter what in a week or so to let me know whether I got the job or didn't. I actually like that he said that he would call no matter what it was nice and I felt it very courteous. I left the interview feeling a bit like I don't know how it went. It started to rain out as I went back to the hood a perfect image to me. When I got back I quickly was into my loser attire and started to have a few beers sitting on my back porch enjoying the smell of the rain mixed with piss and general stank.

Enough of the flash backs but I just thought they were good examples of how hard it is getting good employment. So I needed to go check the mail for the City of Milwaukee's letter letting me know the bad or good news. Hopefully I have met the requirements and will have an interview soon. I know that a letter will be sent because I called the department that I will have the interview with and they said to be on the lookout for a letter that they were not going to be calling anyone. As I drove I was accompanied by great expectation and anxiety with also the hope that I might be able to receive some good news today. Good news or the prospect of having the opportunity for that was welling up inside my soul. Box two forty nine was my box and as I put the key into the lock and turned I was hoping at that time for something, anything instead of nothing. Much to my surprise there was a letter in there from the City of Milwaukee. I gasped a few times and with the butterflies in my chest I held the letter like a mother would hold a child that they might never see again. It was to big of a development for me to open inside the store as I knew that if opened and the news being bad that I might have a break down inside there.

After closing the box and exiting out the door and making my way to my car I thought that this more than likely was going to be very bad news for me. I do not know why I thought this however I can only assume that with all the rejections in life I have had that this would not be a total surprise to me. Entering the car and sitting down I held the envelope on the steering wheel and looked at it like a scientist examining a new found species: with great care and nervousness. Fuck It I say and open the letter with throwing my keys on the passenger side of my vehicle. The sound of the paper ripping open and the expectation was one of losing your virginity, great hope for satisfaction but also great possibility that you will not measure up. The letter in my face with eyes upon it I saw blurry dictation. I was like a child hoping and wishing for praise or the chance of praise. Finally I read the letter and much to my surprise it notified me of the fact that I had an interview on January seventh of 2009! I almost couldn't believe what I read and had to take a minute back and light a cigarette and meditate on this news. As I got half way through the cigarette I looked back at the paper and saw that this wasn't a dream that I indeed had the opportunity of interviewing for a city position. I was so inflated like a hot air balloon making lift off that I wanted to tell the world. Unfortunately this is merely an interview not an actual job offer and thus I am weary of letting to many people know of this good news. Mainly because I might not actually get the job and I don't want people to be let down by this even if their let down might be bad it could not even come close to what mine would be.

Driving back to my dump I was so excited and thrilled and feeling like a child who thinks they are in love. Full of hope and possibility that maybe this might be like the Beatles said my ticket to ride. When I finally got back to my place I stood almost shaking in my kitchen area at the thought that I might be able to restart and be born anew having things working in my favor. I thought about what I might be able to get back the self respect and optimism that I have lost many years ago. Then instantly with all that being flooded into my brain and thoughts I had a negative realistic ninja come up to me and say basically man you are not shit till you have this damned position. The reality of life came thundering down upon me like a weight at the gym you cannot even imagine lifting correctly. With that I felt that it would be okay to notify my mother and father about the prospect of this position because shit they are my parents. Besides that I only told one other friend back in Ann Arbor about the situation.

I wanted to be careful yet very hopeful at the same time. I planned my dry cleaning and laid out my attire even though the interview was three weeks away at this time. I figured I was a high value and that more than likely I would be offered one of the positions available. Now I knew that they were hiring and I called and was told for a few positions so I of course was very optimistic. With that I had to let myself down off the high of hope and seek some more down to earth reality which was in no short supply here in the hood. So I walked over to Bobby's place and knocked on his door wanting to run this proposition by him and seek his advice and thoughts. Now you might say to yourself why would I want to seek the advice and counsel of a drunkard man with a gimp leg right? Well all I can say is that the poor and neglected have great insight into what really matters in this world. They really put things into perspective and let you see the other side of the moon if you will.

Bobby yelled, "who is it", as I knocked on the door. I said, "its Lee playa who else right." After a few minutes I could hear rustling going on in the place and the click of the lock being extinguished and the flash of the door opened revealing Bobby. What's going on he said to me, I was like well I needed a older more wiser perspective on shit do you have any time to kick it I replied in essence. Of course for the most part Bobby never was in a hurry to any place and welcomed me in like the tribes in the bible that believed that visitors shall be protected and nourished when showing up on ones door step. I told him about the recent development with this interview I had and asked him what he thought. He was very enthusiastic about it and said, "damn man you are going to be clean if you get that job." Clean to those that don't know is basically well dressed and doing alright if not great. I said yes indeed and that I was a bit nervous about getting my hopes up about it. He shook his head and grabbed his beer walking in a limp to the fridgerator and said, "man you are lucky to have that problem." I was immediately put in my place with my probably pathetic worries by that statement. Here I am bitching to a man that never had the use of a leg and probably went through hell in life and here I am bitching about my anxiety about a great interview with the city of Milwaukee: I was humbled and ashamed.

With that insight from him like I said it is worthy of some of the best talking I have ever heard from anyone and I said thank you to him and headed back into my place. I realized at that moment that telling your fears and asking for advice from people should be done very seldom and with great caution. That other people have their own problems and when seeking advice or counsel from them or whomever you desire you should take a minute to reflect and be still before making that dive into the abyss of the unknown.

CHAPTER NINE

With Christmas coming around and the constant barrage of commercials trying to get us all to spend money I noticed that my Christmas is not going to be so very merry. Again I am forced on a very simple and poor diet as I am on fumes financially and also with food too. I look into the fridge and see a few hotdogs and some peanut butter and jelly along side some filth of course that has been in there since god knows when. I hate being poor I really don't recommend it to anyone that's fore sure. I feel like as if I committed some crime when I realize that I am basically broke for the next seven days until I receive my next unemployment check. I guess what it is about really is the self questioning of what I probably could have went without, like beers and smoking along with a steady consumption of smokeless tobacco as well. However, these items are definitely essential to my staying somewhat sane as I would like to think. I know this analysis sounds a bit off the rocker but it usually works for me and keeps this animal tame mostly.

And usually when I am pretty broke I do not drink so thus I gain my appetite back to only realize I have nothing to eat. Nevertheless I must figure out how to stretch the few dollars I have and get enough food to hopefully get me by for the next seven days. I believe I mentioned in the novel earlier about how bad it sucks trying to live for four or so days on a seven dollar budget. I am a bit better off than that this time around thank god but just a bit better off I stress. Screw this I want to get out of my place here as this dank air and loathing is really wearing me down today. I also noticed that my loser outfit I have been wearing for I don't know how long now is also below my filth tolerance and I make a personal note to myself that laundry needs to be done upon my return from the store. The laundry is in the basement at this house and I have some weird aversion to going down there. I really find it to be creepy down in the dungeon as I call it. I usually only do laundry once a month lately as I really only wear a few outfits and it isn't like I have anywhere to go or anyone to impress lately. Yes the dungeon area is a weird place perhaps I am being a bit dramatic but it is just one of those places that gives you a unsettling feeling. Looking around the floor I noticed after moving some filth around I noticed some clothes I haven't worn in sometime and thought what the heck put that in the wash pile. I have to pay for the use of the laundry it is a dollar to wash and seventy five cents to dry and to me that is a bit expensive considering to really get one load washed you need to use those machines twice in a row and that would really add up in my mind. Well I suppose I better be off and get this drama over and done with.

When I get to the store I am starting to feel the hunger pains brewing inside me. No not now I yell internally to myself as I absolutely hate shopping for food when I am hungry but also when I am basically broke as well. As I walk up to the store some salvation army person is ringing the hell out the bell and irritating me even more and then he hits me up for a donation Shit I should be asking him for the jar instead I smirked as I quickly passed him by. Going into the store broke is always a bad experience, one that must be done as quickly as possible and with the least pain. Going through there must have been some sales going on for various food products because they had the little old lady's passing out samples of pizza, sausage, and some hi-c of some kind. Of course I made use of all the samples and thought that I was able to avoid a meal for another few hours at least. So I looked inside my wallet and see about twelve dollars and some change. So I figure I would get the loaf of bread for a few bucks to go with my peanut butter and jelly that I already had back at the dump. Next I needed to get some cheap generic style sour cream and onion chips for another few bucks which made me even more appalled when I looked at the name brand chips. My god what is in these things to charge so much? More than likely I will also snag a gallon of milk and then some cheap candies and call it a day. That's right I got in there and out in only ten minutes and I even was able to get some free samples.

This being poor shit is really hard to go through, but I like to give myself a thumbs up with an I get the jobs that I need to get done: done in a timely manner. On the way out the idiot bell ringer is just slamming the bell back and forth and I thought that either he is totally deaf or a major retard to put up with this activity for any length of time. The sun was going down and with a nice cold December evening coming around I figured I better head back and start on the rest of my chores so I can relax a bit later. Trying to get back to the dump as fast as I could I turn on the radio to find much to my annoyance only Christmas music blaring through the air waves. I really wish I could get into this cheer and the same songs I have heard every year but I just cannot do it. Listening to others being cheery only reminds me of the fact I am a pretty miserable prick most the time. I think you have to be in general a pretty happy person overall with few worries to get into this cheesy shit anyway. I don't know I should be a bit more optimistic as the 2008 year is almost dead. I should be elated about that as 2008 has really sucked thoroughly for me.

Pulling into my place and with food in tow I think about the prospects of the New Year and hope that it just doesn't get any worse. I mean the only way this could get even more pathetically bad for me is prison or some terminal disease that would only show itself in a major way forcing me to go to the doctor's office. Yes indeed it would have to be some type of major pain I was experiencing or a sudden passing out to get me into the hospital since not having insurance makes me unwilling to go to the doctor's office and subject myself to the rape of a few thousand dollar bill. Forget that I figured and basically am at peace with that prospect and the notion that no matter what happens medically I will be screwed either way. Let's get some of the jobs done I say aloud and with my index finger doing the number one sign in the air. I really needed to get the laundry done but really wasn't looking forward to going in the dungeon now that it was getting dark outside. Tossing my food into its relative places where I put things I grabbed the load of laundry and braved the dungeon and whatever might be down there. Now it's just a feeling down there that you are being watched it is the feeling that you just don't want to be there and probably shouldn't be anyway. Now I haven't seen any ghosts or have been hit or had anything ever happen to me when down there, but it's just a weird feeling that's all. With the load started I quickly got the heck out of there and back to my room.

My room on the other hand feels as if it is haunted with this damn cold air and no heat. It has been getting really cold in the house lately and I have been using a small space heater next to me at night to try to stave off the effects of no heat but it isn't keeping pace with the cold air coming through. This is really starting to piss me off I swear nothing in these slum houses ever works all at the same time all the time there is always something that is screwed up beyond all recognition. The heat however isn't one of those small things especially in a Midwest winter period and I am contemplating calling the slum lady and asking her what gives. I really dislike calling her and letting her know that the house is a dump because she seems to not care but also not have a clue on how to get anything fixed around this place. I remember me and Bobby talking about a month or so ago and I haven't heard him mention anything to me since so I figure I should see if his testicles are turning into icicles as well.

Pacing around the apartment like a bull trying to kill the matador I feel my incredible hulk like rage swelling up inside me. Not only am I broke for the next week with shitty crappy food to have I am also living in a damn refrigerator this so badly sucks man. The cussing coming out of my mouth with the semblance of some Pentecostal whack job speaking in tongues very frequent and almost unintelligible. I know that if I do get a hold of my slum lady it will be a while till anything is done and I will be freezing for some time anyway. It is one thing to be broke, unemployed, and basically hopeless but when your heating is out to lunch it makes it unbearable and it feeds the rage. The first load of laundry should be done about now as the wash only cycles for twenty minutes. With change in hand I pull open the doors with no regard to the noise I must be creating and stomp down to the dungeon almost daring some ghosts to try to fuck with me right now. Clothes look good enough and I toss them into the minnie dryer and ponder what I am to do about the problems I am encountering tonight.

When I get back I figured I should see if Bobby is home and if he is home coherent enough to ask if he is a popsicle as well. Knock, knock, who's there I hear back on the other side from Bobby. I go the boogeyman man who else open up man its Lee. Bobby swings the door open like a savage and greets me with a snow suit on. I started to laugh and thought how many layers of clothes does he have on underneath that coat. His appearance satisfies my suspicions, but I still needed to hear it from him if I was to bring this up with our landlady. So Bobby you freezing your balls off too I asked him. Hell yeah he replied and limped back inside and sat at a chair and pointed into his kitchen part of the place. Walking in and seeing that it was a bit warmer in here then at my place I looked to my right and saw that the poor bastard had his oven on and open again. What the hell man I say does it help at all? Shit he goes I don't know but I am willing to try anything this is torture man!

Man I am getting really pissed off now that we have to live in such degrading conditions as men. I said let me go back into my place I will turn mine on too what the heck do I have to lose right. So picture this two poor bastards using our ovens to try to heat up our places man what a sight to see. When I go back into Bobby's I asked him if he had told our landlady about this yet. No I haven't I don't want to deal with all her bullshit right now because if she gives me any I might just snap over the phone or in person. I hear that I replied and stood there just shaking my head like a dumb idiot thinking our next move. Well screw this I shouted I am gonna call that bitch and get her ass or someone's ass over here to fix this shit. Bobby was like be careful man, which irritated me even more because like he just told me he has a terrible temper and doesn't conduct himself well when dealing with this garbage any better than myself.

I finally get through to her and tried to start off as the polite douche bag society wants me to be in a situation of being frozen to death. I told her it felt like an icebox in here and asked her if she had the heat turned on as she had hidden the thermometer for the regulation of the heat at this house for some reason. I wonder why now huh to scrimp a few more bucks. She initially sounded a bit concerned and shocked to be honest which helped me to simmer down just enough to maintain my false politeness. Well gee she says it should be on I don't understand why it isn't, how long has this been this way? I said since it started getting cold but we didn't want to complain until it was absolutely necessary and we felt that it for sure isn't working properly. With that little statement out of me she started to get quite catty telling me we should have told her sooner and how she was worried that someone else in the dump might have already contacted the city to complain typical shit like that. Whoa Nelly bubbled up over my head and I said hold on to your britches there little lady. We have been taking this freezing old drafty ass house for a month not wanting to complain.

That seemed to put that bitch in her place and she knew she wasn't dealing with some black old ass alcoholic cripple that could be abused and neglected she had a new sheriff in town and I wasn't going to take this shit for one damned minute more and allow her to do it to the rest of us. Well it is going to be a few days probably till I can get my heating guy over there to look at it she softly now replies back to me. Well I said that's fine as long as in those few days you bring Bobby a space heater of some kind and talk with the rest of the losers that live in this dump to see how they are fairing through this. The conversation ended and I was still bubbling with the gaul of that woman to start getting attitude with me because I am trying to let her know that we are freezing our asses off in this place. I tell you I am never shocked by the bullshit that gets shoveled my way with these slum lords man. They are great at coming and picking up those rent checks boy aren't they but try to get them to fix anything around the place and all of a sudden they have other properties that they are currently working on. That excuse of working on other properties too is total bullshit who do they think I am a total retard?

Walking back to Bobby's I told him about the call and how she was going to get some idiot third rate guy more than likely to look at the joint but hey I guess its something right. Bobby didn't seem to really care to be quite honest he just looked beat down and totally unwilling to complain about much at the time. Sitting there bundled up like he was and me too shivering when away from my little space heater I had on my floor I too was starting to think why waste energy on complaining but then again sometimes being angry is all that one person really has left in life. I wasn't going to let this slide, no in fact I would have to be the point man regarding all this crap I figured in the future because Bobby wasn't going to be much of any help I assumed. Well I went back into my place and stared out the windows in my back and could just feel the flow of that chilly air on my face coming through. It was amazing these windows were leaking terribly and when that heat gets turned on its going to be a huge bill for her. I just then recalled the time I got told I was too over qualified for a job and that she was over here with some man to check if the windows needed replacing. So I cannot imagine a window installer not letting a possible client off the hook when more than likely I am sure he could tell these windows were total garbage. Now I am getting more enraged and again start to pace like a rabid bull around my kitchen. She knew all along that the house needed to be properly winterized for this winter and did nothing I was convinced of it now.

You pay your rent for certain things like a roof over your head and the cable and heat that she said was included and you just want to get what you paid for. I wasn't asking for a new kitchen counter top or more cable channels on our plan or for new appliances even though they were always on the fritz. No I just don't want to pay rent and feel like some of the homeless people freezing outside. I am so sick of being treated like shit by people. I mean I can see the typical jerk walking down the street being an ass to me but having to pay someone to still be an inconsiderate asshole to me must be the norm now I guess.

With my spirit totally gone and my will to even speak sucked out of me I go down to the dungeon and grab my laundry. I was walking up almost in a zombie state at this point because I just don't want to care anymore. I mean it is obvious to me that our landlady probably doesn't care to much or for that matter about anyone else we are all just going through the motions I suppose. Throwing the clean laundry on my one chair in the room I plumped down on the floor and turned on my only source of heat. It takes a little while for this little thing to get kicking but once it does its not bad so long as I don't move. I also grabbed a blanket and wrapped it around me to try to capture all the heat I can and make it warm to the fullest extent possible. Sitting Indian style huddled down around this six by eight inch little space heater in the beginning of winter I cannot help but say I felt terribly sorry for myself that night. I just wanted to belt some tears down my eyes letting the sorry for myself thoughts get the better off me. Alone, hungry, and cold sitting at thirty years old around a little space heater listening to the air whistling in through the windows is very spiritually damaging.

I suppose it is funny how we can be doing an activity as meaningless or mundane as doing a load of laundry and then be succumbed by so many emotions that stop us dead in our tracks. I mean I didn't want to struggle about the fact of my own loneliness or the more important fact that I am living in a virtual icebox tonight. I suppose these things just happen and we are forced to our mental and emotional knees I guess. Sitting and being alone for quite some time now have really allowed me the time to be introspective yet also seeing what the world and others can do to us. I have said this many times but I wish I could be a person at times that is totally clueless to the struggle of the many. I am not trying to sound like a saint or martyr, however I just find those people to be of the most fortunate kind when witnessing them first hand. What good at most times does the knowledge of pain and suffering do for us when we are in a position of total impotence with regards to solving it financially. I guess this old drafty shit hole of a place that I now call my home has let me know that no one cares and perhaps even more frightening neither do I anymore.

There is nothing that I want to accomplish tonight that will make me feel like a valuable person. It is funny though isn't it how actions happening to us can really make us feel like we our mere observers in our own present life and with that realization we want to abandon ship. I guess that's why I wanted to write this little opus to let the world know of my experiences and struggles and not be forgotten like a bag of yesterday's trash. Sitting here and trying to grasp warmth off this damn heater makes me want to abandon ship, rather my ship has already sank and I am merely on a little life raft hoping for a passer by vessel to rescue me would a be more appropriate image. Nevertheless, I will sit this out and still wish on a star that tomorrow is another day like in Annie the musical and hope one day daddy Warbucks will see that I am of some worth. Like I said sometimes all a person has left in life is there anger and rage, but also sometimes some cheesy musical notes that might bring them out of the despair that they are currently dwelling in.

That night was terribly painful for me as I tried to get some sleep with my body going into a state of convulsing from the wicked cold that raped me. Lying on an air mattress which doesn't insulate and inflate was the other bit of bad news I was more than able to experience this evening. I tried many times to position the blanket I had over the small little heater that was pumping hard as it could but the blanket met a slippery fall off it every time I retried this impossible task. Frustrated to the point of no words I went to take a shower if for nothing else to gain warmth not cleanliness. The shower was a nice fix for the time that I was present inside it, however getting out of it was like a wet cold hard slap in the face saying look idiot you are still a poor sorry bastard! Sometimes things in life are just too much to handle, and if I ever hear someone trying to tell me that god only gives us what we can take again I would take that person and let them meet their maker in an unpleasant fashion. With shower temporarily helping me to heat up a bit I headed back into my place and the cold hardwood floor with only the light from the heater to lead my way. Laying there I felt totally left and lost like someone that should not have ever been born with very few options and even less strength to try anymore. So is it right others have it worse off then us and I should just be still and sleep and hope for daybreak right? Something intervened and allowed me to sleep through another horrible evening and for that I guess I will be merely content.

The next few days went by very slowly as I am sure they do to most others when having very little to accompany their time with. Waiting on the so called heat man to come and make things right was of my biggest concern besides my stomach crying out for a real meal. The weather was leaving an enormous amount of damn snow in the parking lot making it almost impossible for me to go to the library or store. The weather in some ways to me was nice leaving others to be screwed and inconvenienced by its showers. The time for Christmas came and went as I do not want to delve too much into the horror that it was for me this year. Let's just put it this way some things even I cannot delve into nor is it really relevant anymore now is it. I was happy this morning to get a call from our slum lady making me aware that some man was going to come and look at the furnace downstairs in the dungeon. I started to wonder if maybe the reason for the furnace not working was the fact it crept people out as well when down there. There I go off in total fairy tale land thinking weird thoughts and at the same time letting the people responsible for this predicament off the hook. No I think they are just cheap skates trying to save a few bucks as I mentioned before. I am pleasantly surprised that she is keeping her word and wait with great expectations that it will all be fixed soon.

Well with 2008 now passed I noticed that the last year was a total disaster for me. I hope in some way that 2009 will be better as I have my interview with the City of Milwaukee on the 7th of this month. I do have my hopes up pretty high for this position and think I should be a cinch for it as from what I could tell I exceed all requirements. Getting a city job would be very fantastic as I have always heard that they pay well and are very hard to get fired from. I mean just look at the garbage workers around here they look like total losers and pretty lazy as well and they are the people I will in part be supervising. Never get to excited these days I have learned because even a job at McDonalds has intense competition and a never ending flow of applicants. I imagine there will be plenty of people applying to this job but I figure with my college education and background experience I should be already at the top of the list. I do not know exactly how many people they are hiring for the job, however I say to myself at least two.

Indeed, 2008 blew royally for me and with this new job interview in a few days I cannot help but be a bit optimistic for a change. A change of pace would be nice having to actually have a normal schedule again I suppose. I would greatly enjoy meeting some new people if I were to get this position and perhaps have a few new friends to go and do things with besides the losers around here. Every time I get my hopes up I have them dashed and I am pretty worried that if indeed this happens to me again I will probably have a total and complete meltdown of gigantic proportions. The weather outside is a total disaster and I can only imagine the fun filled mornings I will have commuting to work if I get this job. I guess sometimes the grass isn't always greener and that to every good thing there is always a draw back of some kind. I cannot imagine being employed again as it has seemed like a lifetime since I had a job. I mean I have been unemployed now for seven months and I question how really ready I am to get back in the swing of things again.

I mean it isn't like I am managing my time wisely really. I don't know how I guess you are supposed to spend a forty hour work week wisely when unemployed. I try to maintain a normal sleep schedule, which I cannot do very well. Sleep is something I either do all day and night or I cannot do at all. I don't know I thought the other day that I might get a gym membership and maybe get in shape, but that is like a fat girl going on a diet to lose weight it just doesn't happen. It isn't like I can run around the neighborhood here to get some exercise not with all the degenerates mucking around here. Shit I probably would get shot or mugged if jogging around here. Who knows really right, I mean you are damned if you do and damned if you don't. I guess I was never inclined much to be one of those self loving guys who masturbate at their own image at the gym. I think to be quite real to the reader here I have made it pretty clear I am not living the clean lifestyle. If though I get this job I will have to get my shit in line and be a good worker bee and somehow I am really finding that a bit irritating to me.

I swear I am a total walking contradiction and I get pissed off even at my own damn self. I want to have certain things yet I don't like what I have to do to get them its maddening at times.

I figure I am just a total unique person then instantly stop myself right in my tracks and say man I am the same as many others, others of whom I haven't met. I thought about the guy who always had the same job for thirty years and never had to think or question employment, and thus not contemplate much about his station in life. Must be nice in some sick way to be a zombie or to be totally ignorant about many things and just worry about the job or maybe also a family. How fortunate I think to myself to not be having to be alone with your thoughts and pain and have all the time in the world to examine ones accomplishments or lack there of. I don't know what I am saying really here maybe a bit of rambling and a bit of actual coherent writing. I guess in this world of everything either having to be black or white it's hard to have to face the facts that almost everything in life is inherently grey. That there isn't one thing that can be totally correct or totally wrong, that there is always two sides of the coin in everything we encounter. I think of being a child again where you believe basically everything you hear and see. I know the stereotype of the child asking why all the time, but I think back to myself for instance where I believed basically everything I was taught. I suppose that is the difference I am finding out in the world and myself that many people still believe what they are taught and not influenced by what they experience.

Anyhow, the day is probably not going to be to exciting as I only have to drop clothes off for dry cleaning and maybe hit the library. I am trying to get the anxiety out of me a bit about the interview and all that being employed would change for me. I was thinking of getting an Xbox game for my console and playing that till my brain is mush maybe that might be a decent activity. I can by games at this store that sells used ones for dirt and probably hit that on the way back from my other errands I imagine. I really think that might be a very viable option for me to do and get out of my head a bit. To be really involved in a game is nice and it's not half bad at making time fly too. I like games that are challenging, but I get really annoyed with the

games that are so hard that you cannot advance. I am not fond
of sport games which basically eliminates almost half the games
from me to choose from. I like war and spy type games along with
the occasional mob style theme in it. Well sitting here on my ass
I get my energy up to go out into the world and face it. Doing
activities always makes me feel a bit better and I definitely could
use the fresh brisk air that is blowing outside today.

As I start driving in this frigid weather I start to hear that my
car is making a terrible screech as I come to stop. Great I have
heard this sound before and make a quick assumption that it is
my brakes that have all of a sudden gone sour. Great another huge
expense that I am surely and totally unable to take at this time.
I try to tell myself that it is because of the weather and that I am
being to paranoid. Wishful thinking is a total waste of time and
just delays the mental breakdown that one will surely have once
reality sets in. I get to the dry cleaners and submit my clothes for
cleaning and as I exit I take a look at my tires to make sure that
it is not them that are falling apart. The tires looked fine for all I
could see, but then again I am not a macho grease monkey moron
so who knows. My little peace of mind that once in awhile I try
to maintain seems to always get ripped totally off the wheels time
and time again.

I figured I better go to the library and try to perform a job
search again when it hits me hard. What am I going to do if
I even get a low paying shit job when my car might die at any
time? If it is not one thing it is many that saying could not be
more absolutely applicable with me. As I get out of the car the
cold wind is blasting me in my face almost to remind me that I
may be a walking bum in this cold weather soon if my car dies.
Going into the library I have such rage that I must be oozing it
off me as even the big bad black boys in there look at me then
quickly look away as if seeing death themselves. I find a fifteen
minute computer that is not used as most of these idiots want to
sit for an hour and just search for ass, leaving the fifteen minute
one open a lot of the time. Monster is where I go to check a lot

of my prospects for employment. Now it really hasn't been that good lately as a lot of the pyramid scheme douche bags have hijacked it lately.

Searching for employment doesn't take long as I am sure I might have mentioned before and with the fifteen minutes of my life pissed down the drain I get up not being able to apply to one single prospect. The car and the worry that it is now welling up inside me is never far from my present thoughts now. Worry is like my second friend besides rage and or maybe depression. When I exit the library I get hit up also by some bum asking for change. What the hell is it with these mongrels that they can take this sub degree weather and beg? I tell you sometimes I think if I didn't have a ounce of self restraint that I would beat on one of these assholes to a pulp for merely annoying me, but I guess I will leave that to the underprivileged with every excuse in the book black man. Getting in my car and driving away I thought that I was going to buy that video game I was talking about and then immediately turned around to my place and went back.

I went back in part because I started to try to penny pinch and also the fact that my car was making agonizing noises wasn't helping much either. Can anything just go smoothly or do I have a fuck me sign flashing above my head? With no game in hand and plenty of time to kill as I return to my shit hole I figured what the hell get drunk some more. I had ample supply available and very little ambition to accomplish more than what I had just done. I started talking to myself and asking questions of how much this might cost me to get the repairs or is it something more serious than just a few brake pads or rotors. Not knowing any of these answers I was asking myself drove me into a complete feeling of impotence. I hate going to mechanics to get my car fixed because I know that they will soon realize I am not a redneck asshole who makes love to my sister and screw me over with the quote. I know for a fact that it will be very unpleasant like a doctor appointment a man makes when he really knows something is wrong and that he will certainly get some bad news.

So my day of thinking well and trying to escape in a more positive way has been destroyed by a damn car. Granted I could be healthy and go for a work out or something right? However, those types of options are a mirage for me and something I cannot or will not entertain. You see when one person is so completely at their wits end they cannot resort to healthy shit anymore it is alien to them because they have been off that self help lifestyle for a while. Pounding on one of these nasty natural light beers and staring out my windows that are letting through all this cold air I am filled with a blank sense of emotions. I am really starting to go numb I think I might have lost most of my capacity to feel anymore as a sort of self preservation otherwise I might go completely mad. Standing there still and rigid as the frozen plants outside I just be still and quiet. With the noise of wind coming through my windows as my only company I stand and stare at some point on the burnt out abandoned house behind my place.

I try to get out of this canitonic state like in the movie awakenings but am still just paralyzed maybe perhaps because I am to scared to do anything in the thought that it too might result in another negative outcome. I hear this crackling noise of metal all of a sudden with a sharp pain in my right hand that breaks me out of this almost sudden slumber I was in for the last half hour. Shaking my head furiously as if I wanted to say no to a crack head bum asking me for change I looked down at my hands. Upon looking I saw that the cracking noise I heard was me squeezing the beer can to complete surrender and the pain I felt was the can cutting into my hand. The little bit of beer that was in the can ran over my hand washing away the blood that was starting to come out of the wound.

Cleaning my hand off and tossing the destroyed beer can away I thought that the ball hasn't yet dropped on me and till it does I should think more positive about this upcoming interview in a few days. I mean I still have a shot at this position and should try to be more optimistic, especially when thinking negative like this is totally counter productive for me. I just hope my car can last a while longer especially if I get this job with the city. Then after a while I might be able with the job to save a bit and get a newer car for once. It is a very vulnerable feeling when everything is contingent on things for the most part you do not control. I mean all I can do is apply for jobs and when given an interview just step forward and put my best foot in front of them. I mean people have to choose to hire me its not like I can force anyone to. As far as the car is concerned I have done a lot of maintenance on it and tried to treat it well, but after so many miles and with the weather I suppose some things just give out and I definitely cannot control that.

CHAPTER TEN

The day of the interview is now here and my anxiety is starting to really mount. The interview is at two in the afternoon and I still have to pick up my dry cleaning with my last remaining dollars. Now the dry cleaning lady that I dropped my clothes off to a few days ago I made clear that my clothes have to be done by no later than this morning and I am hoping they accomplished the cleaning. Doesn't take much to get a guy's anxiety up these days and when I am driving there I keep thinking that they messed up or they will have lost my clothes. I guess considering how things have been going for me this last several months I kind of have a right to be a bit apprehensive about most things. When I pulled up I started looking for the tickets for my clothes as most places will not release the clothing to you unless you have a ticket. My heart is racing a bit faster now as I am ripping through my wallet and am not finding these damn receipts. Where are they? Did I lose them? My interview is in three hours! All these thoughts are screaming at me and my heart is starting to pound like a good coke binge. What's that I see, oh thank god the yellow receipt was behind my Drivers license!

Thank god I say although I am not really praying a lot now or going to any certain church lately. I still am shaking from the encounter just a few minutes ago and am not fully relieved until I get my clothes in hand. I pass the receipt to the lady at the counter who is a different one then I spoke to a few days ago and much to my relief the clothes come rolling on to the front as she punches in the numbers into the computer that controls all the clothes on the line. Everything looks just fine to me and taking my last sixteen dollars I pay the lady and let out a huge sigh of relief as I put my head back and look up at the grey cold sky above. Driving back I noticed that the time is starting to get here quickly and I still have to get dressed and find the location even though I am pretty certain where it is. I push the pedal of the gas and get back to my place as quickly as possible.

I do think I clean up pretty well when putting on nice clothes and having a clean shaved face, but then again what man doesn't look good when dressed nicely. I shaved a few hours before getting the clothes because shaving really bothers my skin and I just hate shaving in general so with that done all I have to do is finish putting on my shoes and head out to find city hall. Now Milwaukee is a pretty easy city for the most part to get around I have found. Milwaukee has a lot of major streets running east and west and with numbered streets running north and south. So with that in mind I grab the address of city hall and think at most it will take me maybe twenty minutes to find it. One thing I was not counting on is that even though on a map it looks easy to get east or west that some of the streets at a certain point are one way and that is not listed on the maps. It is no big deal I tell myself as I have an hour and a half left and decided I would park on a major road that the city hall was on and just walk a few blocks to get there.

All the parking unfortunately was metered and being the broke bastard I am I didn't even have enough money to put in the meter. Now this really sucks I mean the interview they said should take close to forty five minutes and I wanted to get there thirty minutes or more early to be sure I arrived on time. So my car will be sitting for a minimum of at least two hours in a downtown metered area with it showing empty for my time left on it. I am not sure how things work in Milwaukee as far as expired meter parking if they just give you a ticket or actually tow your sorry ass off. Screw it I will just take my chances not like my mind needs to worry about anything more at this time. Getting out of the car I noticed the cold air and also the slushy street and sidewalks as I tried to get to city hall. I am being as quick as I can but also careful because I don't want to show up there with my clothes looking like a pile of shit. I should have found the correct place to park I yell.

There it is Milwaukee's city hall I found it and with around fifty minutes to spare thank god. It is a pretty impressive building about nine stories high and from the inside you can look up all the way to the top I was starting to feel really small and pretty unworthy I must confess. My interview was on the eighth floor and taking the elevator I tried to give myself a bit of an inspection through the mirrors inside and see if I looked okay, and after careful examination I gave myself a passing grade. The elevator opens up and as I walk out I looked over the balcony that would give a view all the way to the bottom and thought I am not in Kansas anymore that's for sure. I found the office quite easily and let the attendant know that I was here for the nuisance control officer job and gave her my name. She must have had at least four pieces of paper with peoples names on it associated with times of the day for at least two or three days as I could barely make out. So upon seeing this I made the conclusion that this was not a sure thing by no means and that there was pretty stiff competition for the job. "Okay Mr. Sanford," she replies "please take a seat you have plenty of time and when they need you they will call upon you, thank you."

Taking my seat I could hardly bare to sit still and after a few minutes I noticed I had around thirty minutes still and so I went just outside the office to better prepare myself. Being quite nervous as this has been my first real interview I have had in many months. The city hall all around me is oozing success and letting me know that I too might be able to attain a bit of it back if I get the job. I turned on my cell phone as to send a few nervous texts to one of my friends from back home hoping that it would take my mind off of the current anxiety. He had a way of putting to rest a bit of my worries by saying in essence that I probably wouldn't get the job anyway and to just go in relaxed and not caring that much. Now he wasn't saying not to do my best but rather have the attitude like when one is about to ask out a hot girl for a date that your going to get shot down. Losing all hope and expectation has a truly calming effect on me. So with that being realized and lodged into my thought process I returned back into the office with a new sense of self confidence.

The time came for the first part of the interview which was a written exercise they told me. I went into this small cubicle type room with a computer and printer and was given a sheet of paper. The lady instructed me that this sheet of paper was a complaint that was made hypothetically of course to an alderman with the city regarding trash nuisance issues. She then told me to write a professional style letter to the person complaining notifying them of what we were doing about the problem and what we were going to do if the problem wasn't solved right away. I like to pride myself on my communication skills a bit both verbally and written and thought that this part of the interview was a no brainer to me. To be quite honest it was, I mean I kicked that letter out with perfect dictation, punctuation and structure as I saw it. The allotted time for this part was around thirty minutes I believe and I had it done within fifteen. Even though I had accomplished it in a timely manner I didn't want to leave anything to chance and thus I reviewed my material a few times before thinking it best to move on to the second phase of the interview.

I notified the attendant that I was finished with this first part and handed the material to her feeling quite relaxed and full of confidence. The attendant being very polite and courteous told me to take my seat again and wait for further instruction. Upon sitting down I noticed a few more people in the waiting room and I started to inspect their clothing and general appearance. One gentleman looked rather professional which worried me some but he had an unshaved face as if growing a beard. I thought man what an idiot he cannot be clean shaved for an interview in this economy because he is trying to grow a beard. My happiness grew as did my smile on my face. There were two others that entered as well a black gentleman and a black woman with him. They must have been together because they were talking as if they were. This guy looked like he came right from some hip hop club wearing jeans off his ass and a regular long black tee shirt. Unfortunately for me he wasn't any competition for me as he was asking for an application for a cook job with the city.

I could see through the glass door and windows that sheltered us from the outside of city hall that there were two chairs in the hall diagonally across from me outside a door. In one of the chairs was a gentleman and he looked somewhat casual not only in his demeanor, but also in his appearance. He was wearing khakis business casual pants with a sweater and he too had a beard of sorts going. I then saw a lady exit the door that he was sitting next to and say something briefly to him as he sat there. She then strolled her way over to our door, and upon opening it looked at a piece of paper and said in a general direction. "Lee Sanford", that is me I said as I rose to my feet I extended my hand to greet her with a nice handshake and greeting of hello. She was a very sexy Latina woman who I spoke to on the phone before and she said, "oh your Lee nice to finally meet you". She then led me to the open seat that the other gentleman was still sitting at and said to wait for them to call me into the room for the oral portion of the interview.

I calmly nodded and smiled and took my seat down by the other man waiting with a look on his face as lets get this over with I have better things to do today. The woman then addressed the man sitting down and told him they would be ready for him in a few more minutes. He didn't appear to me to be of any real competition for this position and I again was starting to think that if this is the caliber of people they are getting I should be a cinch for this. Waiting there with the man to my left looking at all the nice dressed people going about there business was interesting. When I first entered city hall here and finally came to the eighth floor and looked around I was quite intimidated and felt a bit out of place. Now with the incompetence I saw around my fellow candidates I felt much more at home and ease. I saw a few alderman and women being escorted by police officers coming and going and thought man those people will ultimately be the people I will be answering to in some fashion. After a few more minutes passed the door swung open and the woman asked for the man to my left. I knew that this portion would more than likely be awhile so I decided to get comfortable. I also was pretty thirsty and with my mouth being a bit dry I went to the fountain I noticed when getting off the elevator. Walking tall and proud in these nice clothes along with my visitors patch over to the fountain I noticed my reflection in the mirror-like brass doors on the elevator. Man I look like a stand up citizen instead of the man wearing a wife beater shirt with grunge on it and sweatpants that are disgusting with filth.

The time must have went by fast as when I got back to my seat it didn't seem like more than ten minutes before the first guy left out the door. I asked him how it went he was like I don't know with his hands open and out to his side. I trying to get some much needed insider information asked him if they told him how many positions they were hiring for. Going to the elevator he said I didn't even ask. Great, instantly I figured that he probably did a poor job answering some of their questions and also probably didn't ask any of his own either. A few minutes after he left the sexy Latina woman comes to the door and asks for me. As we enter through the door my heart is really starting to pound and no matter how you try to be calm and cool when going into the interview your insides always let you know you are alive. Being cool and calm though on the outside is something I think I can do quite well.

She said that there will be a few questions from each interviewer and to just relax and answer the questions to the best of my ability.

Entering the room I saw three people sitting at a table right in front of me. The person on the left was a white older man who greeted me with a nice smile and handshake. That man made me feel a bit calm and also a little bit less threatened. The middle person was a white middle aged woman who also greeted me but with a look of neither welcoming nor threatening. After the greeting with the middle woman I was back to not knowing what to make yet of the environment I was in. The person on the right was a Spanish looking male probably in his thirties I would guess not much older than myself. He seemed nice like the first man I encountered and being younger made me feel a bit less of a child entering the principal's office to get yelled at by the adults. There was the Latina woman there too alongside her was another white woman just sitting there and smiling at me.

The Latina woman told me that this lady was with the personnel department just sitting and observing along with taking notes on the interview. The personnel lady then told me that she would be writing as I answered but to pay no mind to that, that she was there to make sure the process was fair to all applicants. With all the introductions now being completed the interview started with three questions being asked from each of the three interviewers. I was a bit intimidated I must admit I mean there are five sets of eyes and ears listening and looking at me for any fowl up I might commit. Not to go into the actual questions and my answers as I cannot even recall all of them anymore I felt as the interview was progressing that I was holding my own quite well. The interviewers also seemed to be taking a few notes here and there and giving some reassurance with a that's good to my answers. Now was it that's good as a way to shut one up, or as a true sense of the saying that I was indeed doing well. The interview lasted approximately thirty minutes and it was longer for sure than the man that went before me. After the interview I asked for their business cards so that I may write them a nice thank you note. They all looked as if they heard that request for the first time and told me that none of them had any at their disposal. Well I was even more optimistic now because it seemed to me that they were quite impressed by my gesture and then the Latina lady in charge said just send it to my office. With hands being grasped firmly along with thank you and smiles I felt that thank god the interview was now done.

The Latina woman led me out of the office and said I did well and thanked me for coming to interview today. I asked her when I might be able to hear anything back regarding the job. She told me that they will narrow it down to the top three for final interviews. I was a bit worried by this admission because it let me well aware of the fact that they might be only hiring one person for the job. She said everything is done on a point system and that the written, oral, and past qualifications would all be scaled as to come up with the top three candidates. She also let me know that a letter would be going out to all letting them know there final score with a letter telling them to call if in the top three for a final interview in a few weeks. With that I thanked her again and started out of city hall thinking that I did my best and felt relieved this part was over and that I at least held my own.

Walking back to my car with the cold air and slush I started to think that if they are only hiring one person or maybe two that my chances might not be as good as I was thinking inside there. It was a pretty grey and purple type of winter day being the first week of January. Walking back the wind was coming against me and letting me know that feeling of struggle is never far away. Now with the interview passed I started to worry about parking my car in the metered parking area with no money on it these last few hours. I was really hoping that it would be there even with a ticket so long as it wasn't towed away somewhere. Getting back I saw it was still there and relief flooded my veins, and as I got closer I saw no ticket! Man maybe things are just going to go my way this year of our lord 2009. Being thankful for the pardon I quickly managed to get myself out of there as to not push ones own little bit of luck.

With that big ordeal out of my way I decided I needed to grab a few more beers at the store and reward myself for my excellent performance not like I really need a excuse, but hey. When I walked into the store with these nice clothes I immediately notice that many people are taking a look at my appearance. There really isn't a better feeling than feeling good about the way you are presenting yourself to others and being aware that they too are impressed with the image you are portraying to them. I must have looked like a completely different person to the many regulars I see when shopping there. I mean most times I walk in with my loser outfit on and must look rather beat down. Yes, today was a good day as I have said before. When you are accomplishing something or just in general feeling good about yourself you need to hold on to that feeling as long as you can.

With interview and shopping tasks completed in a most excellent way I headed back to the walking dead hoping that they would not be out and about seeing me enter my place with this attire on. I looked around as I pulled in and could see no people out and so I made my way quickly back into my place fast as I can like the ginger bread man. Setting the groceries down I wanted to get out of my one good outfit and hang it up proper this time as I might have an interview again with the city soon. Placing the clothes on the hangers in my room I thought I should call my mother and let her know how it went as I am sure she is pretty curious about it. I mean when you have been unemployed and a basic bum for sometime any good news a son has should be immediately told to the family.

I called and got my mom on the phone and she was curious to know how the whole thing went off. I tried to be a bit cautious and told her I think I did well however I am not sure how many they are trying to hire. I told her all the questions they asked and my responses and she seemed to be impressed as well. I said that I would hopefully know whether I made the cut for the final three in a few weeks and we would just have to wait and see. I also let her know not to talk it up to much to the other family members because if I don't get the opportunity to interview again I don't want anymore people's hopes to be dashed. She complied and said she would wait to say anything more until we had certain positive information. I was proud though that I was able to give my mother some ray of hope for her son as I have been a pretty down and out man for many months. And much to my thankfulness she has been a real support as of late for me. Although I think anyone with children should be able to understand how hard it is in this economy to be single, unemployed, and barely getting by. I think most would assume a degree of depression with all that. So like a lot of things in life we shall wait and see and hope for the best.

With the waiting game on I have to continue still to try to look for other jobs and not get too discouraged about the whole thing. The next few days I did just that I went to the library and checked my mail. One day when I was checking the mail I found some brochure that had Milwaukee activities one can do in the winter, you know almost like a tourism guide of sorts. As I looked through I saw a lot of things in there and thought I might want to do some volunteer work with some organization. I have always been fascinated by the Special Olympics program and the people that participate in it as athletes. I find special needs people to be the most honest and pure souls walking this earth among the many wolves that we are. I wondered if I might be able to find this organization in this little guide. I went through ever so carefully looking from top to bottom with my index finger on the page as my concentration pointer. There it was Special Olympics and I was instantly happy and saw that there were many activities that they had for these people in the Milwaukee area.

Since it was night at this time I didn't call but I said the next morning I would muster up the will to make a call and see what happens. I marked the page with a pen and circled the numbers that were relevant and wanted to tell someone else about something I was excited about. The most convenient person was Bobby so I grabbed a brew and headed over to his place. Bobby opened the door and was happy to see me and invited me in. He was watching the professional entertainment wrestling that I used to watch as a kid. When I sat down I asked him what that was all about and he said, "Wrestling is my show man I watch it three times a week man". I immediately thought back about the time I was over there and I saw that he was watching bonanza and I found myself grinning and laughing out loud again at that moment. He seemed to be a bit puzzled as to my elation and I basically told him that he watches some cool shit. Indeed Bobby is quite a character always surprising me in some sort of way I suppose.

So I also told him that I had that interview with the city a few days ago and he wanted to know how well it went too. I said I don't know but it felt good being able to be dressed up all nice and clean for a good job for once. Bobby said, "I know that's right man, shit you get that job you will be up and out of here in no time you will be clean as hell." Yes sir, I replied and also told him I was thinking about volunteering for the Special Olympics maybe this winter. That's a great organization Bobby told me and said he could probably have been in it but he felt bad to participate as he thought being of sound mind gave him an advantage. Bobby of sound mind made me internally giggle, but I played along and told him that I would be making some calls about it tomorrow and see what's what.

Watching wrestling and drinking some cold beers was actually not bad as then again I think when drinking anything can seem fun for awhile. Bobby started to go into the characters and let me know the bad ones from the good and his favorite guy on the show. I figured I vented and told my stories and didn't want to just leave after that like a selfish person so I stayed a while and made it appear as if I really cared about the show too. These last few days have brought a bit of hope to me and I am holding on to it the best I can. It's funny that you don't know how sad, lonely, depressed, or out of hope you are until something or someone comes into your life to give you hope and the ability to think of a bright light at the end of the bullshit.

The next day came and I was pretty enthusiastic about trying to get a hold of the lady at the Special Olympics and see if I might be able to be of some assistance at some time. I called and got her voice mail which was a bit of a disappointment but I left her a voice mail with my information and hoped to hear back soon from her. A few more days went by and I had heard nothing back from her and was starting to get a bit nervous. So I called again and this time I got through to her. She acknowledged the fact that she did indeed receive my message on her voice mail and apologized for not getting back to me sooner. I said no problem and we began to discuss the matter more in depth. She asked me to tell her why the Special Olympics, and how much time I might want to devote to the organization. I told her what I already said earlier that the kids in the program are just so happy to have someone pay attention to them that they are a ray of sunshine in this dismal world. She seemed impressed with the enthusiasm in my voice and I could hear her reciprocate it back to me as well saying it's great to have people that think this way. I then went into time and told her my situation and that I would be able to help a few times a week, and I was hoping I would be able to do so.

She told me that sounded great and that first things come first meaning I had to fill out an application form for a background check and send it back to her as soon as possible. The application would be sent out tomorrow in the mail to me and I figured it might be a week or so until all this stuff is sorted out. I asked her if the basketball program was still being done as I saw it posted as one of the activities they do there. Yes it was she said and told me that they actually have tournaments throughout the Milwaukee area and that it is pretty intense. Wow, I thought that sounds really cool and told her I would be more than willing to assist in any way with that. With that we ended our call and said that we both would be looking forward to working together soon.

Hanging up the phone I again was feeling like 2009 might just be my ticket to ride and that optimism like Abba might be taking a chance on me.

What a week it has been I thought, a job interview that I think went pretty good and now I might be volunteering with the Special Olympics in a week or so. It is funny how things can really start to turn around quick when that worm does turn. What pride and self esteem was slowly starting to come back to me. Now being the pretty negative man I have been for sometime I didn't want to bite too much off of the optimism loaf, but I was cautiously hopeful. I ran over to Bobby's and told him I was getting things in place to be able to volunteer and that I would be helping out with a basketball team. Man you going to be a coach or something, I was like probably not just you know do what needs doing more or less. That's fantastic he said and wanted to know what I was going to be doing most of the day. I felt pretty good and said probably have a few beers and find some good TV on to watch. Bobby politely asked if he could join me and if I might be able to help with a few cold ones for him as well.

That would not be of any problem as I was on cloud nine and told him sure we will have to run to the store so we have enough for the both of us. As we drove away to the liquor market which wasn't too far I was savoring the emotions that I was feeling. We got the booze and made our way back talking about how great it would be if I was to get this job and do the volunteering thing. With beers in hand and things going well I enjoyed them and also his company. Loneliness is a bitch and even with some crippled company it isn't that half bad. We started watching Unsolved Mysteries you know the show that Robert Stack used to host back in the eighties and nineties. Now unfortunately they had some new man doing the deed which disturbed me to be quite honest. The shows were all of the time when Robert hosted but now this new guy was doing his voice over his.

I started to remember as a kid watching this show when my dad worked at night helping with fifth grade boy's basketball and my mom worked at some deli job at Kmart I believe. I can remember being terribly frightened by the show and with the lights out almost making it even worst. I do not recall where my brother was during this time which in some way puzzles me. Anyway, the show was on at eight on every Wednesday and I tried to watch every one of them with the ferocity of a dying man at confession. It is uncanny isn't it how simple daily activities can reengage ones brain and make them remember certain things. I loved that show and like many people I loved through out the years they all have now long been cancelled.

As we watched the show and progressed into the evening we started to relax and be more talkative. I asked Bobby what he thought about the show and if he had any good or bad feelings in general. Bobby not being the one to divulge too much information about himself was polite and basically said I have nothing to much to say. I took his response and sifted it over through my brain even though my brain now was pretty gone. Nevertheless, I felt he had plenty to say and perhaps I just wasn't the loaf of bread that he wanted to be a part of yet. I took his polite rejection for talking about himself well and went through the evening not pushing or trying to persuade. I must admit the evening went well watching a marathon of an old show I loved and not being alone made it all that much better. Sometimes I suppose just being in the moment and being with someone else is all the answer we need in life.

The next day after our marathon I went impatiently to the P.O. Box I held downtown to see if I had any response from the city regarding my interview and also the Special Olympics lady's application. Waiting is surely one of my biggest pet peeves and drives me absolutely nuts. With great expectation and hope as I walked up to the box as if a kid again waiting to be picked by the others for a game time activity I noticed nothing in the box. Why despair I thought even though my face if a person there wanting to take a picture of it would see that despair was all over me. Man alive what is taking these people so long I said aloud as I walked back to my car. I mean it has been at least a week and a half now since the interview and almost five days since I spoke with the Special Olympics lady. I swear neglect must be my middle name or something no one gives me any due attention.

Even with the not knowing in my mental handy bag now I am still surprisingly up beat as I manage to drive back to the walking dead. I figured it will be fine and that these people are just busy and all the things one tells him or herself when in total denial. Driving back from the store I noticed how pleasant the weather was and how nice it might be to have someone to go skiing or hiking with in January. Driving and thinking back I remembered the time I went walking through the woods in Michigan's Upper Peninsula with a friend. It was a joyous time for me and the woods being still in their placement were loud to me. I remember the smell of the plants and trees and the sound of air whisking through my ears. The trail we were walking on must have been made for people of smaller stature and barely navigating my way through I found it to be a fabulous distraction. Walking both of us not saying much more than watch out for this or that I meditated on life. Man that walk was so very nice and at the end we came to a lighthouse of all things and I tell you it was so perfectly mundane. There was no one around us to distract our personal feelings that I am sure he also was going through as well.

The wilderness was there for the taking and yet giving me so much in return. Driving back from downtown I felt a big piece of my heart missing that as I recalled this time. I was broken up to the point almost of tears as I found myself gasping a bit for breath as if I hadn't been breathing. Man to feel that free and at one again with the earth was also something I must have been missing and not knowing till just this very moment. I made a point to tell myself that if I was ever to get together with this friend again that we both would do this walk and enjoy it to the very fullest. Pulling back into my place and getting out of my car I again noticed the sun blaring down and reflecting off the snow. It was amazing to me as I was almost blinded by the sunlight at the end of January. The winter is truly a double edged sword; on one blade is the brisk cold air with the purple and grey clouds, and on the other blade stark clear beauty.

As I entered my palace I found the smell to be quite revolting compared to the fresh air I was just enjoying. Window opening would have to be performed and as I tried to do this task I found all the windows to be nailed shut. I have never even tried to open them as Bobby's advice of being totally paranoid had set in well. How troubling I proclaimed and thought what if a fire happened and I would be inside with no way out I might be cooked thoroughly. Well with that option being gone I decided to do the next best thing and just open the door and let the sunshine and air come right in. I mean what the hell it was still day light out and with the cold weather the walking dead weren't to active anyway. What a swirl of wind came into the place as I opened the door I might as well have been in a hurricane at that moment. The long stench of stale smoke, urine, and beer was being evicted from my place as if Mother Nature herself was taking it as a personal priority. What a difference does that make in ones own psyche, I mean the place felt and smelled totally renewed. I took this chance to look outside at the dilapidated surroundings and found that with it in this state was quite relaxing. I mean no one was out and about making a ruckus and to be quite real it might have been a normal suburban type setting besides the burned out houses of course.

The renewing feeling of fresh air was all around and my thoughts started to go back to the unknowing. Walking around in the dump I was contemplating the outcome of the job interview and the Special Olympics. Getting back to reality and the here and now was a bit unsettling as I wished I could remain in the flashback of the wilderness. Pacing and thinking like a caged animal in some third rate zoo my anxiety started to mount even with the fresh air blowing around me. The air as brisk and refreshing as it was in some way made me aware of the present knocking me out of the past reflection. I figured I was at least not half bad off even with the realization of my memory being just that a memory. Hope and optimism must still prevail here and I figured I would surely here some positive news from the city and the Special Olympics any day now.

CHAPTER ELEVEN

The next day came as so many do with no real difference yet I felt that it would yield some sort of news. I arose with the uncanny feeling that I might be terribly let down this day and with that I wanted to be numb and not think. I wanted to maintain my optimism and feelings of self worth so badly, yet knew deep down in places I didn't want to talk about that it might all be easily erased. Gaining my bearing and things I managed to make my way to the door to face the music if you will. Taking a few deep breaths and rubbing my neck with my right hand I gained the courage to open that door and face the world. Still hoping for something profound to happen in a positive way I made my way to my vehicle. Starting the engine and looking around I noticed nothing of any significance besides a few squirrels trying to get a bite to eat. The stillness only interrupted by the sound of my car and the faint sound of music that was trying desperately to get out of the radio that I had turned down. Sitting there with the car on and a feeling of today would be a big day that would let me know if society was willing to give this poor bastard another chance was real to me.

Putting the stick shift in the backup notch it clicked and my car slowly started to remove itself from my place. Still staring ahead with an almost zombie like stare I managed to start on my way to the P.O. Box and face the news. Driving there I felt a weird silence with myself that I can only liken to a dead man walking, hoping for a pardon but deep down inside knowing that it would end poorly. Pulling into the place in front of the store I might have been pulling into a prison facing a lengthy sentence. My heart started to race and I wanted nothing more than to see nothing in my box. If nothing was in there then maybe I could stretch together my self love a bit longer. Getting out of the car should have been an omen for me as I stepped into a large puddle filling my shoes with nasty cold water and snow. Saying the usual profanity I went up to the door and entered as to read my fate on paper. Shakily taking the keys from my hand and placing them in the lock I turned the lock hard and quickly. Indeed a few letters were residing in there and my eyes almost didn't want to look any further. Grabbing the damn letters and shutting the box I walked back to my car to read what information was in them.

I noticed a City of Milwaukee emblem on one and figured now is the moment of truth. Taking my keys I ripped that letter open and started to read the contents. I rated a 93.8 it said and that I finished number eight on the scales. My heart sank because I knew that only the top three will get the chance to interview for the final position. Mustering my strength I continued to read on further to see the plain truth in black and white print. It read that I would be placed on a waiting list for further consideration and to wait patiently for a follow up letter. I knew it god dammit I knew it! There was something in the air that day and I just knew it. I felt like my world was now surely over and with no parachute to pull I hit the ground hard. Sitting there in my car I just went totally limp staring again like a zombie at no one certain object. What the fuck do I have to do to get a decent job or be considered for one? My hands started to make quick garbage out of that letter as if I was in some kind of hypnotic state not knowing what I was doing.

Total and complete deflation was occurring and I was paralyzed by it. Not knowing this at the time but tears must have been running down my face for some spell as I noticed a cold feeling of water on my neck and shirt. I don't know how much time must have passed as I sat there in total renewed defeat but I am sure that I didn't care. The one hope I had been really hanging on was now gone and I was just sitting there in my car with ripped paper and tears to share it with. Totally wrecked now as a human being after the final rejection of me as a person I didn't know which way us up or down, and left or right. Somehow I managed to pull my car out of that damned area and get my self home. Pulling in I still was silent and going through the motions as if I was in some dreamlike state. Once I managed to gain access into my place I went immediately to the fridge to grab me some beer. I saw I had plenty in there and that I was going to be quickly drinking them. Ripping open that tab on the beer I slammed it within a few short seconds. Like a robot on automated pilot I grabbed the second and continued the activity again. With the second down I then grabbed me a third and repeated the task and before a few minutes I had slammed three beers.

Half of the mess still draining down my shirt and the door still left open outside letting in that oh so fresh air I said fuck this to myself. Turning my phone off and locking the door outside I knew that I was entering a dark part of my mind that I didn't want to yet like a black hole was sucked into beyond my control. Like a white man which many of us are and not being able to exact a certain amount of rage in public I felt totally vulnerable. Pacing through my place with an absent sense of purpose I walked and walked looking down at the floor with no real purpose or of any sense of knowing. Being in total and absolute despair and rejection for the thirtieth time I wondered what am I to do? Rage is all I thought and I wondered if I were to commit suicide if I could even do that act correctly. I started to think of how I would do it and do it well with no errors. I started to think that if I were to commit suicide that I would like to make as many people that found out know that I meant business.

By business I mean that I would not be ingesting any pills with alcohol or anything that lame. No I was thinking a duel purpose of me hanging myself on a light fixture then shooting myself in the head before I let go of the rope in the morning hours. I mean what more could be troubling then to some giddy up asshole driving to work and drinking their coffee and seeing a man hanging by his neck with his brains blown out. I mean at least that would be a sort of show stopper in that persons day now wouldn't it be. You being the deprived person that you are and I am not saying that is a bad thing might be asking yourself how can he hang himself and then shoot himself at the same time? Well, I would hold the noose and myself around the light fixture then shoot myself letting my limp corpse hopefully fall completing any odds of error. My despair was total and somehow I didn't want to make that attempt on my life as I thought that even I would probably be to inept to complete the task. How sad is it when you don't feel like you want to be anymore and knowing that you might or more than likely are not capable of ending it. I didn't know where to turn or who to turn to. I was in complete not knowing and I was terrified at what I might do. The sadness was so overpowering and my lack of any outlet was making me come to only one conclusion. The conclusion was to get absolutely and totally annihilated.

With a few beers in the fridge and my mind a total drain with a serious plug in it I managed to guzzle. Tipping my head back and closing those eyes with the breath being taken away I swallowed all twelve ounces of that beer within a few seconds. After the beer consumption went through without any real difficulty I shake my head side to side like a dog trying to shake the water of itself. Staring at the fridge in front of me aimlessly and without care I continued to stare. Staring with the silence of one who knows they are not one. Staring with the knowing that I am incapable of knowing anything anymore. It was like they say in those flights when you are losing cabin pressure, please move your seats to the up right and locked position I was in peril. But what am I supposed to do? I am sure many would like to hear the story of how instantly I was hit by some miraculous sign of divine intervention. No, that wasn't to be the case in this trial more less I was on a wait and see policy as if I was waiting to see if my pardon came through.

After the beer was drunk I immediately grabbed another one and guzzled it as fast as a track runner could run the one hundred meter race, and with steroids. Still staring aimlessly at the fridge I wished for a pause in the mind fuck that was mine. With no energy for prayer and no divine intervention taking place I took comfort in knowing that I was a truly lost soul. A soul with no one giving him a chance nor giving him a hug or ear to talk to. Oh, I am sure you might think that isn't true and that my family and others would do so. Please, please do not be so naïve and also at the same time insult these last few pages. I with the second beer being downed through it in a fit of rage and then proceeded to punch the fridge I was standing in front of. With my right hand hurting I actually felt something for the first time that day. Indeed, sometimes self hurt can bring someone out of the despair of numbness that life had created. With my hand swelling up and looking quite gnarly I felt something, I felt that I am hurting. Now to many reading this they must be like obviously the man is hurting and for him not to be knowing this is terribly odd. No I never said I wasn't hurting, but to feel it physically and see it was a different story for me.

I can remember as I looked upon my hand as it drew all blood and energy from me that I understood why people cut themselves when depressed. It allows one to actually see their pain in the real sense and not in the abstract word of pain. I really didn't realize until this moment that I was actually doing the same thing as if I was taking a knife to my flesh. With this latest of rejections in my file I was letting myself know in the only way I knew how by hurting myself physically. This latest rejection was like someone taking a sledge hammer to a wall and bashing it down. By that, I mean it was showing me how vulnerable and weak I was in not only my mind, but also my body. The sledge hammer blasting away all that made a certain wall strong, and with no real trouble whatsoever. The boom of the connection would not really be of any consequence to me, but rather the opening of the wall letting in the light I didn't want was. Like a child sitting in his hiding place and not wanting to be found the sledge hammer took away what little refuge I had. This last rejection was just that a big sledge hammer taking away from a little child his or perhaps her little hiding place.

My hiding place was my little bit of hope that I had reserved inside of myself. Like a water tower you see in many of the local small towns it now has been depleted. What am I supposed to do with this knowledge and great mind that at times is a burden? The knowledge of knowing, knowing that pain and suffering might very well be here to stay. I wanted to scream out so badly for a god to save me from this pain or rather someone in this world that might actually be in a capacity to help right now. I knew that anyone I might try to ask for assistance already probably had pre conceived ideas of why I was in this position that I was in. I mean they probably thought I deserved this bullshit and with the alcohol they more than likely would think I was just drunk dismissing me right out of the gate. You see, that is where I am at where I have no one I can turn to and even if I thought I could turn to them they would more than likely dismiss me. Still standing with the look of total absence in my face in front of my fridge I again shook my head like a wet dog to shake the mind fuck that just happened in my mind.

I turned quite slowly away from the fridge and looked outside the window. The window was quite frosty and with the cold air running through it still gave me a bit of reasoning. It was getting dark by now as in the winter months in Milwaukee and most of the Midwest it does do such a thing. Walking slowly almost at a step by step manner with my eyes fixed on something, yet not knowing to me personally. I managed to get to the window and with my breath I made a nice sign of me still living on the window. The steam from my respiration and the wind coming through made quite an interesting contrast. Staring out that cold dilapidated window at the desolate surroundings I felt more at one with myself. I suppose if I were to be living in a sunshine filled place with all the beautiful people around me I might feel worse off. No in some way this weather was a comfort to me in some ways. Letting me know that dismal shit is happening to a lot of people right now not just only myself.

Standing there I noticed I was crying again and when you don't know you are crying it means nothing less than you are fucked. The tears just came pouring down as the wind soaking through that shitty window made me well aware. It was like a boxer after a hard fought bout needing a cold piece of metal against his flesh. In some way maybe, and just maybe, it was mother natures way or gods way of trying to take the swelling down. I had to turn away and make my way back to the fridge and grab another cold one as I was not going to let up on this activity this evening. Walking back into my part of my bedroom side I turned on the television to only find that the signal was being interrupted by more than likely the dismal and shitty weather we were having. My Lord I cannot tell you how much this irritated me. I figured in my rage it might just be my box and decided to head over to Bobby's and see if his was working. Taking the remote control in hand and throwing it down like a man playing craps slamming it on number six I headed over to Bobby's.

Opening the door to the center area we shared I could hear some nice smooth rhythmic music playing and instantly I thought, okay he is up. Knocking on his door with a pretty loud and persistent pound I waited a few minutes. Not hearing any movement around the place and not hearing him yelling I began to think he might be gone, not dead but gone away from here. With a second salvo of banging I made my presence very clear to anyone within earshot. Finally I hear someone stirring about in the place and I hear a grumbling voice asking me who the fuck it is. With renewed hope I screamed back through the door my name and that I had a few questions for him. Boom, boom, boom, click and clack I heard Bobby coming and the door soon flew open with the vigor of the wind outside us. What the fuck man, is what he said opening the door, and me being partial to being interrupted in ones sleep I answered politely. I plainly and simply asked if his cable was out also, as we all shared the same satellite feed. God dammit he replied I don't know I am just listening to my music on my boom box.

With great caution and respect I asked him if he may turn his on to see if it is working or not. Now with all the pain I am going through at this moment I just wanted to watch some TV and get away a bit. Turning around and limping with his gate back to the area he had his remote he punched it on. No signal it read, and Bobby being quite far gone said what the fuck is going on man. I said that's why I came over here because mine was saying the same exact thing. With a renewed sense of awakening Bobby started to get rage over the fact that his TV wasn't working too. Oh my god, I exclaimed to myself, what did I open up by this little request? Trying to be very diplomatic and calming I told him it must be the weather and not to worry. Well Bobby being like most drunks once getting rage in their minds it is hard to remove that, and so he continued to marinate it in his mind.

I suppose I didn't give a fuck and with his anger and resentment I was readily carried away. I again was in short supply of caring and understanding. I understood his problem, yet didn't care too much as I was in my own world of shit. As I meandered my way back to my existence I saw nothing that brought me any joy. Getting away from Bobby and all his bullshit and the worlds I felt even more like a total slug. It was like a man watching his hero being crucified and not having any way to do anything about it. I felt completely and totally impotent in my thoughts and actions. I understand how things can make a man filled with rage and disappointment. However, I didn't like the fact of my own feelings. This job I was just relieved of having the possibility for was not in essence losing my soul per say. This job was however everything like losing my soul, mind, and spirit. I wanted to feel like a man again and feel powerful and in some way like America portray men to be. I wanted to breathe and shit fire with no precaution and do so with total and absolute authority.

Sitting here and writing this and reading my own thoughts I cannot help but think I am a mad man trying in some pussy manner to express myself to the world. This rejection of many was to me the shot heard around the world it started my revolution. The revolutionary thought of that I cannot and will not accept the dogma of entire bullshit that is being told to me by my country. Besides walking into walls and thinking life as I knew it was totally over I managed to maintain a degree of normalcy. The talks with Bobby and everyone else that I encountered were nice however they weren't to productive in so far as being mind stimulating. Being so insignificant in life and realizing that has a way of making anybody feel totally like dirt. I am not anything and society has once again told me I am nothing with repeated showings of go fuck yourself airing on any local showing.

Needing some serious medication to numb my rage and feelings of loss I open the fridge and grab a few cold ones and sit out on the cold porch this January. The cold air was not of any real nuisance to me as I was probably colder than it. Hearing the crack and wisp sound of opening the beer I quickly brought it to my mouth and like a desert person needing a thirst to be quenched I downed it with great vigor. I started to tell myself that there might be something just around the bend and to try to hang on to any thread of hope. Better to cling to any bit of sanity I might have in my water tower of hope. I believe I said earlier I would have loved to scream out for some assistance however now thinking about it I don't want to feel even more like a child than I already do now. Pacing and pondering my real dilemma not perceived as some have tried to mention in there pathetic attempts at perspective. I decided to turn on some music and tie a good one on again.

Keep in mind now people it's frigid as hell outside in January up here. I have no friends here but Bobby I guess and I have no real money to go do anything anyway so I suppose I shall wash rinse and repeat my pathetic routine. I heard someone say to me that we repeat in hard times what is comfortable to us even if it is bad for us. As I turned on the TV to get access to my XM radio I had on I got a call from a longtime friend I could see on my cell phone. To say the least I wasn't in any mood to bullshit and say everything is alright and that I am working hard at gaining employment you know all that lame ass bullshit. I let the phone ring and go to my voicemail as I remembered I called him a few times over the last month but you know he's married and has a life of his own you know. I really I mean really despise these married people that when you ask them why you haven't heard from them in awhile they give you that I am married and have a life comment.

That comment is like a weapon of total go get a life yourself asshole. Anyway I figured I didn't want to talk about mundane total garbage talk that is what more than likely I would have had to do in order to have a phone conversation with him. My father is exactly the same way if it's anything to do with pain and suffering on my end I get really quick almost script like responses that are totally inept and not thought through as well as very dismissive. Anyway I do not really want to delve into that right now as I have enough on my plate and as I get my radio station on soft rock no scratch that disco I sit in my one chair and think of my plan of attack for the next few weeks to come.

With my mind actually in deep thought even with a few brews swimming around I remembered the Special Olympic angle that I had wanted to participate in before. I believe the lady said something about the basketball being started for the people soon but I was nervous as if I had missed any meetings or practices. Ding dong, the doorbell rang in my mind of total apathy and I had a string there to hold on to at least it might be something I can do once a week. I did not know what it would all entail or if I would even enjoy it all that much. Lighting my basic light cigarette and pulling quite hard on it with a beer in tow I felt a little more enthusiastic about my situation even though the loss of not getting the city job was still making my heart throb with pain. I figured that in times of great despair there comes great insight and empathy and I was positive that I was earning some sort of non accredited degree in these two portions of study.

I then remembered that I had the brochure thing that I believe I wrote down all the dates and times that the lady gave and frantically arose to attention like a pimple faced marine recruit on Paris Island. Searching through oh I would say a few weeks of unopened mail and garbage mail my anxiety started to mount pretty high. I can feel the thoughts of you jack ass the one thing that might be neat to do and you cannot even keep that in order was running through my head like an Olympics sprinter. Bingo there it is and in not such great shape either I may ad shit all spilt over it and some jelly it looked like making the magazine quite sticky to the touch. Feverishly thumbing through the book towards the back end of it as I recall that's the portion I wrote in I found the string of hope I was seeking. There they were the times and everything listed in my great penmanship and I didn't miss anything at all and my first trial for volunteering was coming up next Thursday.

I must admit when you are in an ocean of total despair and your boat is not necessarily sinking but you are considering jumping off seeing that little light on the horizon is tantamount to being airlifted off an island you were marooned on. Heading to the fridge to snag another one and turning on my stove for more heat I felt a little bit of an opening that I might be of some value still that I might get that yes you can join or be apart. The disco music was blaring in the other room, and my whole kitchen table and floor had the papers and mail that I strewed all over the place. Me standing in front of my stove for extra heat and a smoke and a beer in hand was a sight I felt I needed to make in my memory. Nevertheless, it is hard for my mind lately to be optimistic to much as I feel when I am it is almost like a curse I am intentionally putting on myself.

I really hope that the Special Olympic thing will be of great assistance to not only the people I might be able to help but also with myself more than them to be quite honest with you. I don't think it is a bad thing to help others if it makes you feel good as well especially when you are in the mind hell that is mine right now and in the past. Feeling the fresh air come still blowing quite good through my shitty windows I wanted to go out again and in some way just be. It was nice out there because it was snowing and there were no walking dead to be seen, and with the grayish purple clouds and the darkness they helped create it in some ways mirrored my internal feelings that were going on inside of me. Like in the summer time I really enjoyed the rainy thunderstorms that would come by from time to time because like with this winter dreariness it made me feel like maybe somebody else needed it too thus making me feel less alone in this world. Like I said earlier I believe I was earning my degree in the areas of study in apathy and insight but perhaps I just might also get my masters in solitude as well.

I wonder if my little boat will ever be able to reach a land that will accept me and make me feel like I am apart and of some worth, or if I will just be destined to float around for all time. I believe that many of us in life have and are going through exactly what I am going through in some way shape or form and I cannot help but to think that sucks. I suppose if I do land my little boat on some good piece of land that I will appreciate it all that much more. I just hope that land isn't the same as the land I left and that it will be with others that have gone through the same bullshit so that in that way they will forsurely appreciate it all as well.

Well the day of truth is here so to speak as I will be attending my first volunteer session for the Special Olympics tonight. I am pretty nervous actually as I haven't done anything like this in quite some time and I am hoping that I can find the place first and foremost , but also that I may fit in with the other volunteers. I have found sometimes when trying to assist in these types of activities that you seem to always have one or two people that think they are running the show in a militant manner. I am not saying that it is not necessary to have someone in charge all I am saying is that it never fails that when you have a great cause such as this is that you will most definitely find some asshole who wants to be a minnie Napoleon it seems to me anyway. I suppose I am also nervous too because I don't have much of a self esteem lately and I am afraid that others might be able to see right threw me and say to themselves look at this bum trying to act all citizen like. Paranoia is rampant in me yes it is lately, but do you understand what I am saying the feeling of walking into a situation for the first time and thinking there are going to be people who have some type of attitude and self righteousness. Not the participants that are the mentally challenged no I am not even saying them I am just saying that the so called regular volunteers might make it more of a job than a fun time to be had.

That day I was kind of a wreck and I decided to go to the library on King Boulevard because I needed to get the directions as I didn't know Milwaukee inside and out. Getting there at the library and punching in the address I saw that it was around sixty blocks to the west and I figured it wouldn't be that difficult to get there and that I might want to leave an hour or so early. Being at the library I also figured I would kill two birds with one stone and thought I might even see if there is anything posted as far as jobs were concerned. Of course there wasn't too much there that I saw just a few positions but nothing that I would more than likely be qualified for. After printing my directions I decided that I was going to be able to find the place easily and started on my way back to the dump.

When I did get back I started to think of what the activity was going to be tonight, and that was basketball. With sport you need to have sport type attire and looking around my place I could see most of my clothes lying lazily and dirty on the wooden floor. Oh no I don't know do I have anything to even wear I thought? Then I remembered that I had these Adidas sweatpants that I figured would suffice quite nicely and rummaged through the pile of filth to gain access to them. Having them in hand I then needed socks and a tee shirt of some kind and not I do not have a wide variety of either I just grabbed the cleanest looking tee shirt with minimal staining and a pair of socks. Heading down to the dungeon to do my laundry I was reminded that laundry isn't free and that I needed a dollar seventy five to do this load. Good heavens I exclaimed and set the clothes on the washer and with heavy steps of frustration pounding down on the stairs I went back to my room to even see if I had that.

Now that might seem like a easy task to most reading this, however I must say there are times recently when I cannot even afford a twenty five cent Little Debbie at the gas station! I usually keep my change in a candle box at the corner of a table in the room and upon lifting it I could here some change jiggling around inside it. A smile crossed my face and I was like I am saved hooray! Of course that was a premature conclusion because once I opened that damned thing all that was in there was a few pennies and a couple quarters, but not American quarters Canadian my luck huh. So knowing more than likely that I didn't have much inside my wallet I still managed to look inside with my eyes closed as if in the anticipation of a surprise party. Inside there was seventy five cents, three quarters and I think there also was a dime or two and a nickel so basically an even dollar. As stated earlier I needed another seventy five cents and not having it on me I just came to the bright idea of doing a bachelors trick.

The bachelors trick as I think others have called it or maybe not is basically when you have wrinkled clothes be it dirty or clean and you want to straighten them out but not iron them. You throw them into the dryer for a while and usually that does the trick. The dryer down in the dungeon only required seventy five cents and being that I had that I split the difference and threw my gear in there and hit the button. This is terribly depressing to me that I was not having the appropriate amount of quarters although on the other hand I never really do laundry much these days so I gave myself a break. I had some money still in my checking account maybe around forty dollars so I wasn't totally destitute so to speak it's just that I didn't want to drive out to some ATM and get raped with more fees.

I had a few more hours to go I believe the function wasn't going to commence till around six thirty this evening. With the laundry being done I decided I would also do a bit of cleaning up around the joint as the previous days when looking for the brochure I managed to make quite a mess with all my old mail and the garbage mailings that comes with that. Looking through patiently and seeing that every single thing that was real mail was bills or collection letters from some damn agency. The rest of my mail was those annoying flyers that are like a book thick with all types of coupons and ads my god what a waste of trees. Wadding the wasteful advertisements in hand I threw them into my garbage and managed to actually be able to see my kitchen table probably for the first time in months. After that was cleared I could see peanut butter and jelly filth and I don't know what else was on the table so I grabbed a towel wetted it down and started to clean it off. It looked quite presentable actually and I was pretty proud that I managed to do that because lately getting out of bed is a task for me.

After the table was conquered I set my sore eyes on the counter top near the sink and could see that was in much more need of a thorough wipe down. I mean crumbs and sticky stains the dirt and dust I saw was pretty repulsive even by my standards. With a little elbow grease, water, and time I got that damn counter top looking like a woman cleaned it spick and span man. I had a few dishes that needed tending but that wouldn't take me long because I only have one plate, one bowl, one pot, and one fork, knife, and spoon. I was really on a tear here with this cleaning I mean usually I have to get pretty bent before I do anything like this because house work makes me want to vomit. Wow it was starting to look pretty damn civilized in this dump, however when looking around I could see the wooden floor was just littered with crumbs and filth. I decided a good sweeping might need to be in order as well. I swear I must have had three dust pans that I had to empty into my trash before all was said and done, but the kitchen really looked and smelt quite nice for a change. Now the bedroom was a different story and one I wasn't going to even try to do today this was enough of June Cleaver for me.

Well all that damn cleaning took around thirty minutes and I figured my clothes in the dryer would be just about right. Opening the tiny dryer and feeling that nice warmth coming off of it I reached in and pulled my desired attire out and it worked I tell you the bachelors trick never has failed me yet! I mean I have been using that trick for over a decade now. I had to start getting ready as I had to leave for the function in around thirty minutes or so give or take. I was filled with a bit of nerves as the time drew near for some reason, and I know that its just a simple volunteer type deal and all. I guess its just besides Bobby, my landlady, a few crack heads, and the lady's at the shopping mall I haven't really socialized with real adults who probably have their shit together. I mean a lot of the times I am quite sure of myself in certain situations like this especially if I already know the people somewhat. This for me was like giving a speech back in high school in front of class with the hot girl I had a crush on that was sitting in the front row.

It was not going to be a big deal I told myself and the people were all going to be terribly cheesy and nice and welcome me with open arms and smiles. That sure was a nice picture I was trying to paint for this function and I was a bit proud of myself for doing this. Although like I have said before I am not really into the habit of feeling good about not only myself but just things in general as they all seem to get messed up one way or another. The time of truth was upon me grabbing my coat, keys, gloves, hat, and directions I made my way to the great unknown with some dramatic music playing in my head. I could see on the direction print out as I drove that I would just take capital to seventy sixth street then a left there and a right on the other street and I should be there easily. The drive was going quite smoothly I might add and having my classical music playing I felt like a normal citizen that hasn't been a hopelessly unemployed person.

Once seeing that seventy sixth was right there I hanged a left then a right as per the directions and the school was right there on my right side and I had twenty minutes to spare. It always makes you feel good doesn't it when driving to a place that you have never been and you are unsure of the directions and you arrive with little trouble and even better with time to spare. As I got out of my car I was approached by two lady's with a flyer for some church I guess that was in the area and I politely grabbed it and was also enjoying the friendliness of it all. I then being unsure a bit though of where I parked asked them if I was going to get a ticket if I parked at this side of the road. The lady's were like no its after six as they pointed a bit behind them at the parking sign that was standing there. Now almost total anxiety was gone not all but a good portion and I was starting to think this was going to be a pleasant experience for me.

Heading into the school I was re-checking all my pockets making sure I didn't lock anything inside my car like my keys or wallet. Once that was made an all clear I took a deep breath and as I am about to open the door I had a flash back to my times in Ann Arbor, Michigan for some reason.

I would often frequent bars when I lived there as I had no other real entertainment nor friends and I found it to be quite sobering if you can believe that not in a drunken way but a realization of my true loneliness. I would open the door of a bar and instantly the sounds and smells would hit my ears and eyes like a sledgehammer. The smoke coming off so many cigarettes and the jukebox blaring the guitar like a city's alarm warning of an impending tornado. As I walked in most of the bars I tried to act like I was somebody and that I was somebody that the women or people in general there might want to get to know. I would order a beer or two alongside with a water to keep me hydrated as I would more than likely be tying on a big one that evening. Sipping or rather guzzling beer after beer down I would try to make some small talk with the person next to me or the person at the jukebox. I would find this to be a great example of how I was totally invisible to these people.

I mean as the night would go on I would be looking all around me at the tables and see a group of people that clearly knew each other and they would all be laughing and having quite a good time. I would see at the door when it opened a couple entering and holding each other tight like first time lovers do and with their lives in front of them looking delightful. Indeed It seemed I always walked into a bar by myself into a almost club that people already had company to go with them. They all were looking at me and the music stopped like what the hell loser, you came in by yourself? I would sit there throughout the evening and my loneliness would be just pouring over me like the bartender pouring her thousandth drink off the tap. With my beer and smoke being my only friends I wandered why I would even come out to a bar in the first place. I felt so foolish and embarrassed by the fact I was sitting in these bars by myself probably looking pretty pathetic.

I guess this is what I was worried about when I was going to open the door to the school. I know it's not a bar but it is like a club atmosphere and I was the new guy showing up all by myself. I was worried that they would give me the same what the hell are you doing here look that I got at the bars back in Ann Arbor. I must push on and I said to myself fuck it and opened the door and walked on through to the other side. As I entered I could see a table with a woman sitting at it about ten feet away and we made eye contact. I smiled and she asked me what I needed and I politely told her that I was here to volunteer. She seemed to be quite nice and said great there are a few people already practicing in the gym you can go right ahead. That was a load off a bit and I walked in and there were two other volunteers and a few of the kids playing.

I introduced myself and said I was there to help out and the guys were very nice and said well we can always use it come on let me introduce you to some of your players. My players I thought to myself what? Anyway as I was introduced to these incredible children and a few were adults as well I felt important and almost like a rock star. These people were so warm and excited to meet me grabbing me by my hand and leading me to this or that it was fantastic! I have to tell you the mentally challenged people if that is okay to say are my kind of people so warm and kind and not judging nor expecting anything but your kindness, attention, and time.

I started to try to play myself a bit and boy it reminded me that I haven't played basketball in ages. I mean I wasn't even coming close to the damn hoop I felt like one of the kids that is so un coordinated that he couldn't probably even raise his hand up straight. It brought a few laughs from the kids and the volunteers as it was quite a display of very un man like talent. Nevertheless, I didn't let it discourage me because for the past several years I have been sitting either on my ass at work, a bar, or at home so I didn't let it worry me that much. As the evening progressed and others showed up I could see it was a decent grouping we had going here and that it might be a bit of work more than I had anticipated. I had to tell myself that I wasn't there for my entertainment or amusement really but rather there to be of assistance and actually help out. My mind of me doesn't allow much more thinking of other possible scenarios but I was reminded as soon as the practice started up.

The lady I was speaking with the last few weeks arrived as well and seemed to be very nice and happy to see that I actually showed. A mother of one of the kids too was present and helping out and her son just kept giving me a big smile and staring at me it was kinda funny actually. She tried to tell him that it was not a polite thing to do to stare but I started to think that he might not have seen new people helping out in some time, or that's at least my assumption of the situation at hand. The gym was pretty small and reminded me of the times as a child when I played basketball at the school gym. We started out by getting in a circle and stretching out and that made my back and hamstrings cry out for a reprieve. I am so stiff I suppose sitting on the floor or sleeping on it because my air mattress was deflated almost all the time didn't help with my flexibility much.

They did that count thing where you hold the stretch position till ten and then rotate to the other limb and I couldn't even come close to holding it. Of course everyone else was doing it with no great degree of difficulty and I just tried to not cry out in agony that loudly and get through it. Stretching that was something too I hadn't even needed to do or thought of to do to be quite honest. The things you notice about yourself when placed in different situations can be very revealing to ones own reality. After we got through the basic training as it felt to me we started to get set up to do some drills you know passing, dribbling, shooting, the typical practice activities. We started by doing a defense drill first where the three volunteers would get out on the three point line and dribble into the five kids that were playing defense then throw the ball to the other volunteer. I wish I would have been advised as to the brutal force of defense I would be soon encountering by these kids.

I caught one of the passes and did a little dribble in and was swarmed by them and being man handled like I never had been before in sport. Gasping for breath and a line of sight I managed to get the ball off to the other volunteer, but man I was sitting there going I am gonna get killed here. Of course I am not meaning the kids had any malice of for thought about that I mean they were just terribly aggressive and wanted that damned ball badly. I started to regain my composure and when I met eyes with another volunteer coach he smiled and said welcome to the NBA buddy. It was hilarious I was for the first time in quite awhile laughing genuinely and not thinking about my despair. We did this drill for awhile longer and I got the hang of what to do and what not to do. Basically, dribble once and pass quickly do not try to enter the defense at all as it was totally un passable.

After that it was the lay up drill which I was happy to hear and knowing that the physical contact would at least be limited for now. As the children made their attempts at putting the ball in I couldn't help but laugh a bit because to be honest it was totally not happening. I caught myself quickly and used a perma grin and clapped and said good try but it was hilarious. The kids on the other hand were all business and no jokes or at least for a bit until they would smile and laugh, although some when missing the hoop would say a few words and be angry the rest were good. I vividly remember this one kid or maybe he was an adult I suppose, but he made most of his lay ups and when he did he would scream, "where's the milk at!" Where's the milk at I thought scratching my head in total bewilderment? I looked at one of the female volunteers and she was smiling and showing her hands with palms up to her side going I don't know either.

Where's the milk at? What a kick ass saying I started to think as I heard it over and over from this guy. So completely and utterly random it could only be a totally kick ass comment that I would have to use at some point in the future. We continued that drill for a while then did a team's type thing where there were two teams of kids with one coach volunteer on each team playing a game. I cannot remember what we played up to or if we did actually have a score we were even keeping at the time. With our little colored vests on over our shirts we picked teams and sure enough me being the new guy I was selected to one of the teams. Now after the lay up drill which I also participated in a bit I could tell I was taking some deep breaths in and was so out of shape. I wondered how I would hold up playing these kids with the energy of a truck going down hills with no brakes able to stop it. Not being deterred or being lame I set out and said to myself, "where's the milk at man?"

The other coach was trying to teach them the plays they had been trying to learn it sounded to me and I was quite impressed with there attention at times to his instruction. Then a second would go by and one of the kids would grab the ball and start running in the opposite direction without dribbling man that was some serious traveling. I smiled and thought I would so like to be that kid just grab my life and run in another direction than society was telling me to try to go. It was a spiritual feel there I felt and I really was enjoying the atmosphere and the laughs that I know would help me out through that night. With a few of the kids being pretty high functioning we managed to run a couple of the plays and the milk was definitely good.

After about ten minutes we switched teams and coaches much to my relief as I was totally spent I mean totally. I was developing a good sweat for the first time in a while and was trying to play it off as I went to the water fountain. Watching the other teams playing and seeing the joy that they were having along with the joy I could see from the coaches made me feel that this is what life should be all about. Simplicity and joy with no one keeping score just everyone working together towards a common goal. No one person the boss and no one person the slave worker. The game went on and I was just enjoying it a few parents also seemed to come in and watch as well with pride permeating through their entire beings. They seemed so happy and proud of there sons and as I made eye contact with on of the couples I could see their thanks in their eyes for us helping out the great kids. I guess sometimes in life some things just don't need to be said aloud.

The games finally ended and we rounded up and the coaches said lets thank coach Lee for helping today and all the kids to the best of their abilities gave me a loud thank you, it was very humbling. After that the coaches said here's the schedule for some upcoming events if you can join us and I of course said I would like to do that. As I left to go outside I could see the dark night ahead and the frigid winter air hit me in my whole being as I was pretty soaked with sweat. Getting into my car I made sure I didn't drop anything in the bleachers and started to make my way back to the walking dead and review the evening a bit.

Driving back I was pretty proud of myself for taking the chance to go to this function and get out of the ghetto and experience something different. The dark cold night all around me and the city lights lighting up clouds and smoke stacks in front of me was quite interesting as well as far as painting the mood. It didn't take long for me to start feeling the effects of this volunteer work I just did and I could tell that I would be in for some serious aches and pains come tomorrow if not sooner this evening. Taking my right off of capitol and then my right onto Locust I stopped at the BP gas station on King and Locust. Getting back into the hood was interesting as I had to regain my don't fuck with me look because we cannot be all smiling here no sir. My thirst was enormous and I snatched up a big Powerade I believe it was a blue colored one and guzzled it down with no time to spare. Getting back into my car and finalizing this trip back to my place I felt the loneliness of it all being back here and the feeling of what am I to do now?

Well the mind kicked in first for once instead of my emotions and I said take a shower and clean up a bit is a start there Lee. With exhaustion I was walking pretty slowly into my place as I was indeed very sore now at this time. It was funny I was walking like the walking dead very slow and with a grimaced face on. I laughed as that thought came threw my mind and setting the energy drink down I just stretched a bit with hands on hips leaning back and tried to just take it all in. It was an interesting night and I also got that great quote out of all of it, "where's the milk at?" Being in this funk all the time I grab on to anything that lightens the mood. It was a great evening one I wanted to remember and I didn't want to do anything but sit down inside my room first before showering. I sat down in my chair and just looked at my surroundings with no noise but the sound of the cold air outside whistling through the windows around me. It was a nice sort of stillness that I felt one that made me actually feel relaxed not uncomfortable. The night was over and I was just sitting there pretty content, of course alone and tired, but pretty content, yes sir pretty content.

CHAPTER TWELVE

Well contentment doesn't last to long in Lee's world lately and the facts of this existence are bearing down upon me with great force. The food shortage I seem to run into often is again here and I am well aware of the fact that I don't receive any more unemployment until a week from today. This really sucks not having enough food to eat and not being able to qualify for assistance because my huge unemployment that I receive disqualifies me from getting any of it at all. Yes, isn't that funny I make too much to get any assistance considering I am living in the hood in a shit hole surrounded by total degenerates. I look into my fridge and see that I am more than likely going to be out of food if you even want to call what I have food in a day or so. So the question begs to be asked, what the hell am I going to do for the next five to six days? And even at that if I do manage somehow to get buy till then will my unemployment be deposited in that correct time or will they fuck it up and make me wait even longer?

I have talked to a few people in my circle, family and friends alike and sometimes I hear the total lame advice of just get a job at Wal-mart or some place like that. Okay let me tell all that my unemployment basically amounts to a job that pays ten dollars an hour. Of course with taxes and SSI and all that shit it does or would come very close to what I am netting at this time. So when dumb ass pieces of shit tell me to go to work for seven to eight dollars an hour it makes me want to beat the shit out of something. Because if you do go back to work you are legally and I think to some extent ethically obligated to make the state aware of the fact that you are working again. When you do let them aware of that your benefits get cut and you will no longer be on the pay roll. It is so mind numbing for me to try to tell these idiots that fact and I think to some extent they like to see someone else struggling and that they get a kick out of pushing my buttons, which at this stage would be a button on a nuclear warhead.

So do you see my dilemma I am in as far as that is concerned? Also I have been applying to god knows how many jobs, and many of them are total waist of space jobs that pay ten to twelve dollars an hour so even if I were to be accepted for one of those positions I would basically still be in the same position financially that I am in now. And when I do apply for these low rent jobs I don't even get an interview because I am told I am over qualified which I am, or I sometimes have even received the rejection email that says my qualifications do not meet their requirements for a damn customer service job! It would be very humorous if it were not so pathetically sad. I believe I described earlier in the book my great encounters with the so called staffing agencies in this area. So I mean I have tried to have others assist me with getting gainful employment however those douche bags were just playing solitaire on their computers and collecting a measly check for all I can tell.

Standing in front of this fridge and seeing the dismal supply of food that resides inside of it makes me want to cry and then break something with my fist. It is truly a sad site and not only that the Special Olympics are having another function in a few days and guess what? I won't be able to attend that because I will not even have enough gas to get there and back! The little voice in my head tells me to call and ask for a ride or something like that. Well come on now I don't even know these people and second I live in the hood and am miles upon miles away from the place we need to go. Sometimes you just get sick of telling people that you are broke or are in a very tight place financially or emotionally. Man this is going to be a very long week I tell myself and then I come up with the idea of stealing to get a bit of food. I have done it before usually hot dogs are easy to snatch and they can help you get by for a few days anyway. I hate stealing it really makes me feel like a total and complete slug however I don't have a choice at this time. I sure as hell am not going to strong arm some old lady and rob her so I figure this would be the best out for me.

Facing the fact that I am going to be going to the store to try to snag some hotdogs I just ask myself what the fuck is this coming to in this country? I have a college degree some decent work experience and have applied to tons of jobs and cannot get an interview for ninety nine percent of them. The only interviews I got was with that car dealer and the city, and the car dealer one was a total nose bleed but the city was the only good one I have had in six months of being here in Milwaukee. Well I must go on right, and head out to the store and try to not get caught at thirty years old stealing fucking hot dogs how embarrassing is this. Indeed, I believe my total self esteem is now and probably will forever be absent. Getting my clothes on and snagging the keys I open my back door and am greeted with a load of snow blocking the door. I look and see that my car and the whole parking lot is in like three feet of snow and am totally amazed.

I haven't left my place for a day and a half or so and being that I have my windows totally closed off so the walking dead can't look in I must have not noticed that we were dumped on recently. Rage flowing already now is bursting out like a rabid monkey escaping from the zoo. I say that's great, just great, and slam my door allowing a good bunch of snow to also be sucked back into my kitchen. Dammit, so I throw off my gear and figure I would go over to Bobby's and ask him what the hell is going on as if he will know either I sort of thought. Knocking on his door I could hear the music blaring in there like usual so I thought one of two things, he is up and around and might not be able to hear me knocking, or he's passed out again. A third and then a fourth knock I rap on his door and finally I hear signs of life.

Kicking the door open quickly and with a, "what", I say "Bobby man did we get a snow storm the last few days?" He was like hell yeah man where have you been? I said, "I was just watching movies on my TV and hanging out I hadn't left in a day or more." Yeah man he replied we got like two feet last night and the airport even was closed. I asked him about the snow plowing here as when I looked out our alley way was packed as well as the side street from what I could see. He told me that you are in the hood man and that they don't plow these streets until the last they get the major roads then the nice neighborhoods and ours later. I was completely getting pissed off at this time hearing this information. I then said, "well what about our parking lot, doesn't our landlady provide some help clearing all that shit out?" Bobby laughed which to me there wasn't anything funny about this situation and said, "that she doesn't do shit like that man."

He said the previous landlord was a guy and he always would come buy and plow them out but since he sold it to her a few years back she leaves it up to the tenants. This is just great another mind blowing peeve of information. Back in Ann Arbor the city did an excellent job of snow removal on the streets and alley ways from what I can remember. I then remembered the guy upstairs that she told us during summer was going to be doing the lawn cutting and snow shoveling. I asked Bobby about that, and again he just laughed saying that he and her had some history and that for all he knows he's working his rent off in a different way, as he winked and winked again at me. This just plain and simply sucks man I mean I cannot get out of my parking lot because of all this damned snow I am like a prisoner in here. Bobby being so beat down in all his years just took this shit in stride and it didn't seem to bother him not the slightest. I wish I could be like that but I cannot be I suppose I expect something out of people and life still, how foolish is that idea beginning to sound in my head lately.

Life sure has a way of telling you how insignificant you are in this world, and if you think you are someone that isn't replaceable I would like to say that you are. So being inmate number s9999 I went back into my room and tried to think about what I would do for the rest of the evening as I had no beer and very little food so it was going to be quite agonizing. I am thinking really about the Special Olympics function that I am going to miss in two days and how that really makes me feel like a pile of compost. I really wanted to go however considering these storms and all even if I had gas I cannot get out of my place and drive there. The one thing that I actually enjoyed is now in jeopardy of being a thing I can do again or at least in the near future.

I had some eggs left in the fridge and some miracle whip so I figured I would make a bit of egg salad to try to get my mind off of these latest frustrations. I had a half loaf of bread left so I figured I had a few sandwiches I could make and survive on till the weather broke and the roads got paved hopefully. Hunger is something that really hits me to the core of feeling like a human being. I know that my hunger experience hasn't been that long just about a year it has really been hitting me, but it really is affecting me in ways I cannot really describe. It isn't just the physical craving of something to eat really it is the mind set that creeps in on how to get that physical feeling to go away. As I said earlier I am going to have to try to steal some hotdogs at the store. I mean it is madness what hunger can do to you. I really feel a great deal of sorrow for those in Africa and even probably staying just next door from me who are suffering hunger on this cold dreary night tonight.

And I am sure many people say well you piss money away on beer and so do the others in the neighborhood and if you spent it more wisely you wouldn't be suffering so badly. You know that is an argument worth making and to some extent I do not object to that. However many people might not drink or smoke but they spend a shit load of money on fast food and the like. Since being in this depressed living area and job market sometimes one needs to escape through alcohol or drugs to just try to keep sane. Now

I am not endorsing that lord knows if I could get by just watching TV all day and not feel stressed out that would be great, however it just doesn't work that easily for me and I am sure many others. I am tired of all the judges out there and their naïve judgments about me and the people surrounding me. Come live in our shoes for a few years and see that every door that you are trying to open is being slammed shut in your face. You try to live in our shoes a bit and on a dismal amount of money to buy overpriced food and then you might get that pompous arrogant attitude checked a bit. It is so true that you cannot relate to people unless you experience it. You might think you can, but you cannot and I thought I could until I went through this living hell in a bigger way then before and realized that I was a child in my knowledge of pain and suffering and that I really was naïve.

With the next Special Olympics function coming up in a few days I knew that I would have to cancel and not be able to attend due to my lack of money to pay for the gas to get there and back. This was not an easy thing for me to do but I felt I should at least call the director of the event and let her know that I would not be able to be in attendance that day. The only thing that I had to do now was come up with some excuse that would be believable and not make me look like a total degenerate poor man. I figured since I was unemployed that I would tell her I had a job interview back in Michigan and that I needed to give it my best shot considering the lack of opportunities that were out there at the time. So with quite a bit of apprehension and anger I called and luckily I got her voicemail which to me was just fine. I left her the message and hung up the phone and was really frustrated at the whole situation at hand here.

Life though is like this isn't it things happen that are sometimes out of your control and means to do anything about. I wanted to be thinking in that way as the usual thinking or rather reliance on my emotions was getting me absolutely no where. It was mid February by now and I knew that the Special Olympics basketball would be over in a few more weeks. In some ways I wish I would have started sooner and planned ahead for it better so that I could have participated more. Knowing my financial situation and that most of the events were quite a drive away from me I came to the bleak acceptance of the fact that I would not be able to assist anymore.

I thought to myself that it wasn't all bad and that when I get back on my feet some day is the key word here I would help out again and not be in this money crunch of a position. Just then I heard someone knocking on my back door and when I opened it there was Bobby. I asked him in and told him of my situation recently and he seemed to be very understanding about the whole thing. Bobby usually is as he has gone through his share of disappointments and frustrations that of which I hope to never equal. The Special Olympics organization is a great one and I hope that I get a job soon so that I may be able to go back and really give it my all. Bobby said that he wanted to watch some TV and wasn't too much in the mood for listening to my thoughts on all this any longer. I could tell he had been drinking and that also was fine by me and I too needed to get my mind off this hurdle that I was not able to jump.

Bobby especially likes to watch those survivor shows on lately and to be honest I think they are pretty entertaining as well. Bobby of course needed a beer and I went into the fridge to grab each of us one. Sitting there watching some guy eat bugs in the middle of a jungle was a nice way of getting my mind of my latest problem. Bobby loved to say that most of the things these guys would eat might not be that bad. Me cringing and wanting to get sick and laugh at the same time I managed to hang in there. It was nice when Bobby would stop by usually it would be me making the first effort to get him out and about. We had at that time I think it would be safe to say would be considered friends to some extent, or maybe some might say drinking buddies. I though on the other hand would like to consider him my friend.

The next week was going to be a go get them week for me. I made a goal to myself to really get up and at them and try even more aggressively to look for employment. I wanted to go to the library every day and try to look in the phone book as well in the business section and look up different companies on the internet and see if they might be hiring. Since the staffing agencies here were pretty lame I figured this might be another approach that I might be able to take. I must say this job searching and applying jazz is exhausting, and just when you think you might have found a good fit for yourself and apply a few days later you get the rejection email. Sometimes you do not even get the rejection email back so you just sit and wait hoping for something to come along one day. This economy is awful and the jobs and the pay for these jobs are even worse in my opinion. As I am sure I have mentioned earlier in this book about how hard it is to get an interview even let alone a job now its months later and I am still in the same boat.

My television died a bit back and my mother was gracious enough to give me a gift card to Wal-mart so that I may actually be able to get a new TV. When I was there at Wal-mart I started to make conversation with this big African American man about this and that and told him about my interview I had with the city a few weeks ago. Now this was in January when I met this guy at the store not now at the end of February. Anyway turned out that this guy actually worked for the city in the housing department I believe. I shake his hand and told him I was hopeful just waiting on a second interview and much to my dismay he reached in his pocket pulled out his wallet and said here take this. He handed me a card and on it was his contact information for his department. He said to me to call if I was so unfortunate as to not get the other job and keep in contact with him as he might be able to dig something up for me in the future.

How fantastic I thought to myself and very caring and generous too. So this week I was going to send him another email and see if anything had come up. Yes, I had a bit of an injection of the go get them attitude which when I get it I better get off my butt and do something. Some people from the upper part of Michigan would sometimes also let me know of some jobs that might be opening up there too. I thought that this was a very nice thing to let me know of; however I just didn't want to move up there because if the job was to go caput up there I would be stranded because there are really no jobs worth speaking of there. Nevertheless, I was gracious and thankful for their looking or if not looking keeping me in mind when seeing something they think I might be qualified to do. That Monday I was ready and had my go get them hat on and even though the weather was still pretty cold outside I wanted to walk the few blocks to the King library. I really felt that maybe at the end of February things would start to turn as I have often felt in the past and to no avail.

This was going to be different though I exclaimed loudly in my optimism that was coming out for the first time in awhile. As I walked into the library I saw that the computers were open and I said see look today things are going to go much smoother now young man. And upon looking on the usual suspects of internet sites for job postings I didn't really see anything that would be for me as far as my qualifications. Again, many of the jobs were either brain surgeons or burger flippers nothing in the middle so to speak. No that wasn't going to get me down I went again on the city and county websites and searched them again hoping for someone to have quit or got fired. Now as far as the city or county jobs were considered I was willing to do about anything because of the benefits that I would assume they would carry. Many of those jobs have great pension programs and that was something I was more interested in than some garbage 401k.

Unfortunately, I didn't see any jobs on there either that I would be able to qualify for as I knew I was not able to do water purification treatment engineer jobs. It was shaping up to be the typical job search that I have run into many times in the past. I also wanted to check the Milwaukee Journal Sentinel Sunday want ads in the paper and so I found the paper in the library there and thumbed through it slowly. Looking through the paper it didn't take long as there was only one page of ads present and most were nurse jobs again or trucker jobs. Man I would be a trucker if I was a big brutish redneck type however I am not and so that would not be a match for me. Still trying to stay in optimism attitude I said that I shall not be discouraged and go back to my place and look through the phone book and write a few business names down and come back and see if I might be able to find them online. If not I would just call them and plain out and ask if they would be hiring soon.

Walking back from the library I remember it being one of those nice brisk yet sunny Midwestern type winter days. The sun shinning out ever so brightly and yet still the cold air brushing my face with the sight of my breath enveloping my head as I exhaled. Even after the disappointment in the library the weather outside was so refreshing to me. I mean the other surroundings were not to pleasant to look at considering I was in the hood, but the cold air made me get a renewed sense of keep going and just enjoy the walk back to your place and take it a bit at a time. As I approached my back door I saw my neighbor Carl outside doing a bit of shoveling. Now Carl is a huge black man very muscular and all that, but he has been one of the nicest men I have ever met and always gives me a waive from his car or a hello when we are out and about. I always admired him because he seemed to never be wearing dirty clothes. His clothes were always the whitest of the whitest and the brightest of the brightest. I even told him I was impressed, and he laughed it off and said thanks.

I told him sometimes you gotta let people know they are working it you know. Anyway he asked what I was up to and I just said man trying to apply for a decent job if I can find one. He said he knows what that's like as I knew he had a job but I knew too that seeing his car he probably barely was getting by just like everyone else in this country. Carl made quick work of that snow in his drive way and then he asked me who was plowing ours out once in a while. Oh that's right I forgot to tell all you that my landlady eventually got some guy to come over and plow out the driveway a bit but only after a huge down pouring of snow.

Anyway I said to Carl that the son of a bitch is doing a half ass job because he has been plowing at an angle leaving like two to three feet piled up behind my car and another mans that lived up stairs from me. He said that he knew that was right and wasn't all too happy about it. I asked him what his beef was about the plowing.

He said this bastard when he went from the alley way was leaving his plow down and was then also leaving a two to three foot barrier of snow at the end of his driveway. Man I said I don't know the bastard that she picked but I told him I would mention it to her and also said that if he wanted I would go get her number and he could call her himself. I then mentioned to him that she wasn't too great at getting constructive criticism and that might just be a waste of his time. Carl with a big smile said thanks brother I just hate how this guy plows he said he doesn't need to be dropping the plow through my part of the alley way. Thus plowing me in all he has to do is pull the damn plow up for six feet and the problem would be solved. I agreed totally, with his view and told him that the guy usually comes at four or so in the morning as I have heard him a few times before. Well Carl said I work nights remember and I cannot confront him then. Oh that's right I said, well I told him if I ever hear it again I will let him know and I would also mention it to my landlady it can't hurt you know. Much love Carl said and I told him I was getting cold and needed to go into my place to look through the telephone book for businesses that I was going to cold call or look up on the internet. We passed and left but I always really enjoyed Carl he seemed like a good person to me.

Getting back in my place and feeling a bit energized I sifted threw some of the papers that littered my kitchen table to find my phone book. I also of course noticed that I would need a pen and sheet of paper in the plan that I might be able to write down some possible leads. Looking for these two things in my place was going to be a difficult task to manage as I felt like a person on an important call needing to write down a number and never seeming to have the pen ready at hand. Bringing in the snow now melting all over my floors I figured if anything maybe these wet shoes would be able to grab a sheet on the floor if nothing else. Finally after about ten minutes of throwing things around like a tornado hitting the prairie dust I found what I was seeking out. Going back to my table and with my left hand clearing away the debris I grabbed the phone book and got started. Now this isn't as easy as you think to do when looking for jobs. When I got to the business section I could see a lot of names of businesses but then again really didn't know where in proximity they were to me as not all had the addresses listed.

Proximity is an important thing when you are driving an eleven year old car with over a hundred thousand miles on it and in the cold weather up here. Also when you don't have a dime for a new vehicle or the savings at your disposal proximity becomes even more a consideration. So I finally said check the yellow pages at least if it was a company of some size they might have an ad and a little map also located in the ad that might make it easier for me to find. Thumbing through I saw a lot of the typical business types at hand and I felt I might have a few with maybe a aluminum recycling place maybe they have a office and need help. I found a metals type factory all of the companies that seemed of some size were pretty industrial types and I felt that if anything would be available that the office type position probably wouldn't be one of them. Getting more discouraged I still took down a few names and then remembered that I applied to a job with a cable company here and sought there number out. I found it not in the yellow pages but under its name in the regular business section.

Calling the eight hundred number I was in the world of the run around automated system which was getting me angry. Listening to all the prompts and hoping to hear one that said if you are inquiring about a position or positions available press here. No there were no such prompts detailing me to do this and I felt that I must in some way be able to hit zero repeatedly and get a human being. Pressing for a minute I must have given that automated system a heart attack and it led me to an actual person my god! The lady on the phone sounded like she was in a terrific mood; no I am seriously being totally sarcastic. Anyway I made my inquiry to her as to what I needed and she was like look in the phone book. I trying not to let my rage meter rise even more like it did with the staffing agencies or when on hold with the unemployment dolls said that I did and all I could find was this triple eight hundred number that was listed. Hearing her sigh and her total lack of concern blaring threw the phone she said well there should be a listing for all the separate offices if not call back. Now this is exactly the thing that pisses me off royally about some of these people that companies put on these so called help lines or customer service areas. These people should not I repeat not even be let out of their houses with their attitudes.

I asked her if she might just be able to give me a few listings right now seeing as though that I had her already on the phone. I don't think that was a difficult thing to ask. She said she could find them right now and would look and if I call back she might have them ready by that time. My god what a mess anyway what was I to do I had to try to look again through the phone book. I already knew that I more than likely would not be able to find the other street office listings. What the hell I suppose it isn't like I had anything to do today of any great importance either right. Looking back at the book I was trying to find it again and sure enough she was right and there were some street offices listed there. I saw one for Martin Luther King Boulevard and that being close I figured I would inquire there. I believe that was one of the offices that I was able to select when I applied on-line.

Calling that number was much easier to get through however I received another woman who was equally sounding less than enthusiastic to be taking my call this afternoon. I politely told her that I applied to a customer service supervisor position a month or so ago and was curious as to if they were still hiring. She then with a brief silence came back and said you need to call the eight hundred line at our corporate office and inquire with them. For all I know this woman wasn't even listening to the question that I asked and with the brief hesitation in her response she was probably doing her nails. I know in her defense she must get these calls all the time, however it still is her damn job. I told her that I tried to get through on the eight hundred line and I didn't hear any prompts that would have let me do any type of inquire mode. Sure as shit she just said sir you need to try again there is a way to do it. I then said okay with my rage ready at this time to bust out of my polite cage. I asked if she might be able to go over quickly with me the proper numbers that I might be able to hit because I didn't hear anything remotely that was for what I needed.

No sir I cannot, she replied, and with anger now being let out from her with no problem. I knew that asking for a supervisor was totally the wrong thing to do because nine out of tens times the supervisor is going to be a raging lunatic as well and thus I would pop off. Also I figured that if I was to ask for some idiot supervisor I would be put on hold for hours in the system I just knew that would be the outcome. Like I said earlier I am unemployed and have nothing to do today which was true, although trying to get information regarding employment and if they have received this or that just makes my day go straight to hell in a serious way. So if you don't succeed try and try again right? Boy would I love to be in a room with the asshole who thought of that great quote. Dialing the eight hundred number again I remembered the lady I was talking to before and her saying she would try to find the information for me if I was to call back. This is more than likely a huge system what kind of chance is it that I am going to get this lady again and also that she would even be looking anyhow.

Man I was really feeling like a total douche bag right about now and I knew that things were going to just make me even more upset. The system kicked on and there I am listening patiently for a prompt of job inquiry or something that might resemble my concerns that I was looking for. Press one for this and two and so on and by the time the number nine came around it said for a repeat of the menu press nine again. So it gave eight prompts and the ninth number was to repeat them and the zero was for the ever so polite and helpful customer service or what ever they were called. I hit zero again thinking just maybe I would get the same lady thinking that many people that were trying to get this type of information already would have put a bullet in their heads and given up. At last I get another one and I couldn't tell if she was the same lady as they all sound so terribly angry to be answering the phone. I asked if she was the lady that I spoke to previously about inquiring on the status of my application. No sir, it wasn't me and then just plain silence, I was like okay well can you help me with my question?

No sir you have to go through the prompts on the menu before me. Rage boiling now I said well there is no actual listing that says for application and job position inquiries hit this number they all are for new service or discontinuing it, trouble, outages, things like that I said. She said then I don't know what to tell you sir have a great day and then ended the call on me. Saying a few choice expletives I pounded my fist on the table and damn near broke the poor thing. Then a moment of Zen came in and said in a nice little voice why would you even want to work for a company like that and more than likely with these types of lazy incompetent people? I thought true that is correct they would more than likely give me a coronary very quickly then I screamed like a psycho person, " because I need a damn job that's why!". Taking some much and seriously needed deep breaths I just sat there staring like a zombie like I often have been doing over the course of this last year. I find that helps if you do it and just concentrate on one point and try really hard to be numb.

Well I could tell that was a total waste of my time and especially in this day in age when everything is apply on-line and every time you try to actually talk to a decision maker you get his type of run around. It is so frustrating and demoralizing when looking for work. I mean this type of system I know is probably needed by these big employers because of the shear amount of resumes they receive, but it just makes you wonder then who is actually getting through this maze of shit to actually even get a call for an interview let alone even get the job. I don't know I am not the Zen master and do not know these questions for which I am seeking the answer to. Just plain and simple most companies are like this now I mean I just get automated email rejections in my hotmail account that is a standard type deal. Again, again I know that to expect a certain amount of personal attention in this type of thing is a huge thing to expect and I do agree, unfortunately when you have been unemployed for almost a year now and receiving nothing but these responses it is a bit different I think.

The job search is over for the day and maybe for the next few as new postings on line rarely are getting changed in the area when I have been looking. That reminds me I was watching fox news the other morning and they had some bitch on there that was saying that on line looking isn't the way to go and that you need to get off your ass and go into the place of employment you want and ask in person. And she was saying that news papers in addition were basically out dated as a way to look and people just needed to start doing more networking and being more proactive. First, I fucken hate those two words when applied to job hunting, networking and being proactive. I mean as far as networking is concerned I don't know at this time of anyone who is working and the few I do I know that they wouldn't want to help me out anyhow. And being proactive my God what a punch word I mean they mine as well tell me I need to be more enthusiastic. The word just doesn't mean anything to me and I guarantee to many people right now in America who are barely getting by. This lady however was selling her book and wanting to basically tell the American people you are idiots and lazy and secondly buy my redundant punch line word book that doesn't help you do anything but lose money on the purchase. Sorry I don't know where I went there, oh yes in another rage filled flash back that I too have been experiencing a lot over this last ten months of looking for my next job, and doing it ever so little proactively and not net working, what a crock of garbage.

Chapter Thirteen

Well as I woke up this morning in the middle now of March I started to reflect on how fast this time has gone by that I have been here in Milwaukee. I cannot believe that I have now been here for seven and a half months, my goodness, and have accomplished nothing accept learning more about the effects of poverty and the shame that comes with it. Looking for a chewing tobacco that I like to chew and my towel I headed into the bathroom to take a much needed shower. I enjoy showers but prefer a nice bath from time to time but seeing as we have just a shower I have to make due with what is before me. The shower and bath scenario is kind of what I feel like I am in right now just accepting what is being set before me and with no real power to exact change through my own efforts. My efforts too I feel have been pretty big in a lot of ways and I feel I have tried to find work and do the best that I am able to do at this time. Anyway turning the shower on and letting it run for a while as it takes a few minutes to warm up I looked into the bathroom mirror.

Looking back was a man that has seen some hard days and even worse nights. Although my eyes showed as far as I was concerned a man needing to excel and have others let me do it. You see in America today the old saying of you do it yourself and if you work your ass off you can do anything is totally a myth nowadays. Looking at my own reflection I knew that deep down inside that I could try to manage my life in a more healthy way probably and try to be more up positive. I think that I just have to look around and that is so wishful and to be honest unrealistic for me to accomplish at this time in my life when everything has been turned upside down. As the shower was heating up it started to produce the steam that was now starting to erase my reflection in the mirror. That is a nice way of how it feels to be me lately when I try to excel or look ahead and even at myself there is always some outside force beyond my control that blurs that goal or image for me.

With that mirrored image now gone I went into the shower in search of cleanliness but also hopefully some sort of divine baptism. The shower was so small I mean pathetically small as if for a five foot tall Neanderthal or something. Trying to move my arms to wash my hands I was greeted by the dirty shower sheet clinging to my body and it was quite unpleasant. Anyway what's a little bathroom grime from time to time right? Standing there trying to get a bit cleaner than I was before I entered and also not to catch any disease I started to think about the future. A lot of my time since coming to Milwaukee has been more reflective and not really looking forward in many ways. Well it wasn't total looking back I mean many times I could barely stand the present, however I really started to think about the future. The future is a difficult thing for me to even try to dwell on as I thought coming here was going to really produce some new job and some great new friends. Of course that never did happen so far and was looking more and more like it was not going to anytime in the at least near future. Cleaning myself and allowing the warm water and the soap to clean off some of the smell of smoke, beer, and body odor off me I started to feel renewed. Renewing in my sense of thinking that I might not have to be totally stuck in this rut that I was in here.

After the shower was done I went into my room and sat down on the floor and just took all my surroundings in. Not seeing anything that I would like to see much longer I also though was painfully aware of the fact that I was financially unable to change these surroundings. I think many Americans today are stuck in this same rut and have no real way of getting out of it. And once you lose a decent paying job today in America you have to painfully come to the realization that you might not ever make that kind of money again. That I think is what has been so difficult for me to accept and deal with. I mean I was never making any real kind of money ever in my life, but knowing that now I might not even make that again has really made me angry over this last year. I want to be more positive and think better about this country, others, and myself but life sometimes doesn't allow you to lie to yourself. The job market in this country is horrible and for all intensive purposes I believe that America is also over.

Like I said earlier no longer can you pull yourself out of poverty and make it, shit now you are born, live, and die in poverty no matter how hard one tries or what race you may claim. Those bastard republicans though would have the American people thinking that with lower taxes and tort reform we can manage the economy and healthcare. These idiots are so out of touch along with many democrats I must confess also. I don't know I wanted to be more positive today and not dwell on the facts of life as they currently are, however to not acknowledge them is to not know how to get around them. I think many Americans and even myself to some extent do not want to think, that's the key word here think about why we are getting screwed over so bad. I believe that if we had a society of people that did or I should say could think that we might never have allowed all these dammed crooked business man and politicians to fuck us with no lubrication for this long. It is so frustrating to see my countrymen and women accepting so little out of life that it makes me sick.

When I hear people that are working for ten dollars an hour or less say at least I have a job I want to beat the shit out of them. Yeah a poverty slave ridden one if you will please. I too have had to accept the exact shitty paying jobs in my life I have never had a job that paid me more than eighteen dollars an hour in my entire life and I even have a college degree. I must confess I have no idea about my future now that I started thinking about it. You see I told you I can barely stay in the present and then when I start to try to be all positive and think ahead I am hit back with the facts of this life and country. I mean we as citizens really have no real recourse against this huge machine of capitalism and the greed and corruption that it creates. Yes, I suppose many of you reading this might think that, hey I have a vote don't I? My god yes you do but between Beavis and Butthead, both choices are just terribly unacceptable but that's all we are allowed. My rage is building again when I think of how bad this country has really gotten and how terribly hard it is just to survive fuck even think about raising a nice American family.

Well at least I accomplished something that I can look at this afternoon, I took a shower! Yes indeed, I think that is what I come to when thinking about this life and this country be happy with the little mundane aspects of our pitiful existence. That's just it though I don't want to be someone who is just existing. I am not such an over zealous prick that I want to rule the world and have ten cars, a yacht, and my own island either. I think many of us Americans just want to have a relatively comfortable life with a decent family and home and a job that cannot be taken from us. Oh oops, I almost forgot when I just wrote that last sentence, the problem is many Americans DO in fact want to believe they can have everything and pay little. Sorry I started to be too idealistic and not realistic in some of my writing and for that I apologize. But seriously most Americans do want to be responsible and live within their means.

Wow, I feel totally drained with that last rant and I now start to understand why I just like to get drunk a lot because if I think I go crazy. Middle of March it is now though and I really want to see what I might be able to do as far as if I am going to even stay in this city or if I might move back to Ann Arbor or somewhere else and give it a go. I did start thinking about that too while I was in the shower about maybe just moving again and planting my flag back in Ann Arbor again or maybe some new city. Now Ann Arbor I was having a hard time with finding decent employment after losing my job at the bank I worked for back in May of 2008. In addition to that the rent levels in that area are quite high and I do not think I would be able to get my own apartment there on ten to thirteen dollars an hour no I know I couldn't afford it. Then if I did move back to Ann Arbor I was thinking I would have to rent a room again like I am sort of doing here and that really sucks I have done it before and hate it. Also, the Michigan economy is the worst in the country right now and I don't think that jobs would be easy to come by there.

Ann Arbor is a beautiful city that I love and it is sort of like my home now even though I am currently living in Milwaukee. When my parents divorced several years back the house I came to know as my home was sold and my parents sought new accommodations. I guess seeing as though I lived in Ann Arbor for around six years it was like my home, not a home away from home but rather my hometown now of sorts. Then again I can remember before I left it to come out to Milwaukee I was ready to leave because I couldn't find any work and I knew that when my apartment lease ran out in a few months I would not be able to afford another place. I knew that and knew that I would have to go back to room rental again and that idea made me crazy. The idea though of starting over in Milwaukee sounded like a pretty damn good idea and I figured that even if I had to do room rental again it could yield a new and better beginning for me. I wish I would have known how bad a part of town I was moving to before I did, but hey you live and you try to learn right.

The idea of staying here where I am at in Milwaukee isn't sitting right with me much these days. I am really getting fed up with all the blight and apathy that I see everyday around here it is truly depressing. I think in fact the apathy in some respects has been influencing me a bit and making me not expect much out of life anymore too. I mean coming here to Milwaukee's north side and living around all blacks as a white male is interesting, but it also is very limiting too. Limiting in the way that they really do not want to get to know me and in some ways I don't want to know a lot of them either. Milwaukee is a big city and I suppose I could start looking at the south side or to the west where many suburbs are and find some better lodging there. The west part of the city did seem pretty nice I had to drive out there a few times to interview with the douche bag staffing agencies which was a great time.

One of the most difficult things for me being here is that I haven't met any people and I wonder if I would if I stay. In a better part of town where I might be able to meet people that aren't strung out or violent might help of course. And maybe if I did look out in those areas I would be able to meet some people that actually have jobs and be able to point me in the right direction, you know network! All these things could happen anywhere I guess and I just really don't know what I want to do right now. Moving really sucks and I hate it, the good thing is that I don't have shit to move really I mean no furniture or bed my bed I can just deflate. Then there is always the idea of moving to a whole new city that I have never lived in before too. With my finances being pretty tight as usual and thinking of my car I would hate to be driving a very long distance and be stranded out there somewhere with no friends or family within driving distance. Also I don't even know what other city I would like to move to that might offer me a decent rent level and better job opportunities. You never can tell when you just pick up and move to a city especially when you have never lived there before. So I guess I will just take it easy as I can and wait it out and see what comes along in this head of mine.

What a day this has been a lot of thinking that is for sure and as night draws near I try to exhale and take a bit of a breather. The night in winter is always a nice thing I think. I like the somber feeling that it reflects like a mirror back to me. I went in put on some music and grabbed myself a cold beer along with a cigarette.

I took a seat at my kitchen table and lit my smoke. Cracking my beer and taking a big pull off my smoke I took it all in this day. The beer tasting mighty good and I felt like I just got done with a really good counseling session in some way. Even though this life is very frustrating for me and the present times are producing nothing of substance I feel that I still in some way am alive. I get terribly angry and filled with an insatiable amount of depression sometimes, but hey that happens to others too not only myself. Drinking this cold beer on this cold winter night I felt like I did accomplish something today, and not just a shower.

I accomplished the fact that I might be looking to go somewhere else then this place on the north side of town and maybe just a move might send me in another direction. I have known people in my life that have never moved or have never had a different job then the first one that came along. That is a nice thing I imagine to have, but that is not going to happen for me now and maybe ever. I have to accept these things and try to understand myself and also the situations that are out of my control. Accordingly, I will be thinking and absorbing all I can in everyday that is going by and try to enjoy what little bit of winter is out there. I have often had people ask me if you could do it over again would you? I think in life sometimes there are things that happen to you and no one person can avoid it or control it you just manage it the best way you know how. This cold day in the middle of March was one that got me thinking at least and maybe even planning a bit and I think that that is a good day.

The following week I received a call from a good friend of mine back in Ann Arbor named Kevin L. I believe I referenced him earlier in the book he was my friend that was having some trouble with his marriage and also the fact of being unemployed didn't help much either. I always enjoy my conversations with Kevin because for once I felt that someone actually not only knew what I was feeling but was going through a lot of the same things at the same time. He of course was in distress and was not enjoying the weather back in Ann Arbor or the terrible job situation. I told him I totally agreed and that things here in Milwaukee were not shaping up to be remotely looking positive in that respect. I mentioned that the other week I was trying to be more positive and think about my future more. Of course he kind of laughed at that being very pessimistic about any of our chances in this economy.

I too engaged in the laughter a bit as it was hard for both of us to think in a positive way any longer than a few minutes. On the serious level though I mentioned that I was starting to think about moving either back home or to some other part of Milwaukee as living amongst the walking dead just was getting to old and to dangerous. I told him that my unemployment extension would be running out in June and that if I was going to make any changes even a little move that I would have to do it before then otherwise I would be stranded in the hood working at Burger King. Kevin then broke into some ideas that he was floating around in his head as well. He stated that he was thinking about moving out of the country and for good. Kevin a year or so ago went to the country of Panama to visit for I believe ten or so days and really enjoyed the atmosphere that was there.

I can remember him telling me how cheap everything was there from cigarettes and beer to the women and lodging. I too was very intrigued by this notion of moving out of your own country in order to establish yourself and have a chance at a better living. Anyway Kevin said that he was this time looking at Nicaragua instead and said that the lifestyle down there is even better than Panama. Of course I had to inquire as to the legality of it all, you know passports, police corruption all that stuff. He said that it would be no different than Panama and that in fact it might even be a better idea for him. Well not ever wanting to be the one to piss on others dreams I encouraged him and said shit here in America it seems worse than there. Kevin feeling reassured by my comments seemed to take a deep breath that his friend wasn't going to give him the typical rebuttal that I am sure many had already given him about his idea.

I wondered how neat it might be and also how terrifying it would be to move to another country especially one that speaks a totally different language. I asked him about the language barrier as I felt that would be more of a concern than anything else. I mean if you cannot communicate what are you actually going to be able to accomplish while there. Kevin never one to not have an answer said that he was learning it and picked up quite a bit when he was in Panama a year or so ago. Kevin then said that of course this plan was not going to be an immediate decision that he had a child and many other things that he wanted to work out before he would seriously consider it. I guess to me it was more like a lot of my ideas, having many but never really acting on them. I planned to be supportive to his dreams as he has always been very supportive of most mine. Though when he did give a sigh of disapproval at some of my ideas I suppose now looking back that he had a good right to do so.

Kevin is such a breath of fresh air for me when we talk because it isn't bound by the typical American strategy. What I mean by that is that we are all taught to be in this cookie cutter form and to utilize the same straight line to so called success. You know graduate high school, then go off to some college or university and maybe do an internship somewhere and then boom land a nine to five job for as long as you can. With me and Kevin we thought totally outside the box about life and how we felt we could achieve an actual life style that was fitting to our needs and wants. Kevin then asked me if I was seriously considering moving back to Ann Arbor or if that too was another passing idea. Well I said I was and in fact it still is a chance that I may stay here but I just wasn't too sure of what to do next with my life. Most of life lately in the last year wasn't really going anywhere and I didn't want to make another rash decision.

We continued our conversation about more of his idea to really look at Nicaragua and see what he might do when there. He mentioned about starting some strip club that would also sell juice drinks and have video games there. Okay people you see how his ideas can be totally outside the box? Anyway I still thought it might not be a bad gig because when you involve naked women and alcohol it usually ends up being a total disaster. Plus he added that by not providing alcohol he wouldn't have to go through all the chains that you would need in order to get those permits. Kevin mentioned something similar to me back a few years ago when we worked together about doing something similar. So when I remembered that I figured that this just wasn't a passing idea for him that it in fact was pretty serious to him.

I told him that before he would go down there for a more permanent move that he would be well advised to go down there a few times before to scope out the area. Kevin of course agreed and said that he was starting to go online and get more information about the city that would most likely be his place of business, Managua. And he did have plenty of time as of late to inquire thoroughly about this venture as he was unemployed and pretty desperate for something. I asked him if he had thought up a name that he might use whether it be a Spanish name or an English name. He said that he wasn't really set out on one or the other that he would let the type of business set that when the timing was right. I am a sort of consultant now if you will and say that he should try to go with something Spanish as he was going to be in a Spanish speaking country. I could hear him getting more and more excited as we discussed this venture and that brought me a lot of joy.

I told him how I always would have loved to have my own business too. He then reminded me of the time I did when we worked together. Yes I started an office cleaning business and I was the president, accountant, sales manager, and worker. The business I felt was a good one to start because the barriers to entry were little as far as start up capital. I saw at the place I was working at how we had a cleaning service that was being run by a bunch of guys from Uganda and how shitty of a job they did. Now the kicker was that I knew the accounts payable lady and I one day being very curious asked her how much we were paying them. She with a kind of I shouldn't be doing this look at me but also with a smile of this shall be fun pulled the information up. It was absolutely stunning how much we were paying this company for a once a week cleaning. So each month this company would only do four cleanings and all they seemed to do was take out the trash and vacuum and even at that it was suspicious. Finally, the amount of the monthly payment that we were cashing out to them was four hundred dollars!

I at least thought that was a considerable amount because our office wasn't that big at all. I figured at most it would take them three hours a week at most to do the shitty job they were doing and that came to thirty three dollars and change an hour! My mind now was in full I can do this mode and I started to think of how I could accomplish this. Well I got an attorney and set my company up and also got the business insurance and felt I was on my way. Also I did get some professional business cards made up and all for around a thousand dollars. To make a long story short it was a total disaster. I finally was able to convince the lady at my work who made the decisions regarding who we hire for the cleaning to let me get a three months trial. Now this lady was always pretty anal but I thought that since I was a co worker and the like that she would cut me some slack at least the same amount that she cut these other incompetents that were doing it now. Boy was I wrong this lady rode me like a jockey riding a horse with whip and all. I mean everyday I came back after a night of cleaning there was this and that I didn't do I mean it was horrible. After my three months were up I said screw you find the old guys again. I was really upset by this and felt like man I just wasted a grand.

Of course I recited this story to him too and he was like yeah that was a decent idea but man too bad it didn't work out. I mean it was I thought if I could get just eight places at 400 a month or a few that were a bit cheaper that I would be making more money than I did at my job. And I even tried to do a mock work week schedule and if each place took three hours at eight businesses that's only twenty four hours a week and of course I would have all days and most nights to myself. How naïve I was though I mean starting a business is easy any nimrod can do it but making it successful takes a lot of work especially more than twenty four hours a week. Kevin was sympathetic to what had happened to my idea and I think at that moment he too was starting to realize that it would indeed be a lot of work.

Changing the subject a bit with him from that I asked him about his kid and if he was maintaining some sort of fatherly presence. Kevin said I try to but I cannot handle being around my wife. I was not surprised by that comment as many men often say that but I asked him why anyhow. Well he started and then paused as I could hear a guzzling of beer going on. She just ridicules me and makes me feel like a bad dad because I'm unemployed. I told him that as long as he is looking and trying that she cannot even say those things. I mean god Michigan is in a really bad recession along with the rest of the country what does she want you to do get a sixty grand job that easily. Thanks Kevin replied, and said I know but it is that man thing in me a bit to provide and take care of my child. Of course it is I told him but I think at this time just spending time with your son is of great value to him. I mean I also said that he needed to pay and help out all he could and he told me he was.

I swear me and Kevin were like two pees in a pod both thinking and experiencing very similar things. Kevin then switched the subject back to me as I really couldn't blame him. He asked me if I had been applying to anything recently and going to the library on a regular basis. I told him that I had been going to the library a lot and planned to go later this afternoon but wasn't finding much to apply to recently. I told him that man of the jobs that were initially good I applied to and either got rejection letters in email, or didn't even hear back from them. The other not so desirable jobs I had applied to most of them including jobs that paid as low at eleven dollars an hour. I could tell he was feeling my pain and I too now wanted to end the conversation because I was getting a bit frustrated. I told him thank you for calling and that we would be talking more often and that I needed to go to the library.

That was a nice talk though I felt overall and it is not like we don't talk a lot already I just felt that this was a good one. Looking around for my coat and shoes I could hear Bobby in the hallway. I went out and said hey Bobby what's happing man? Oh not much he replied I am just going to go back to bed I had a late night last night you know. He did look a bit tired and rough and I told him I was going to the library and asked if he might need something later. Bobby being the somewhat independent type said no and that he would holla at me later. I hadn't seen much of Bobby lately it usually goes like that with us, he does his thing, and I do mine and then we hang out for a few days. Finding my gear and getting ready to once again search for jobs I also thought that I might include doing a room search in Milwaukee and also Ann Arbor. It was getting close to April now about a week away and the weather still being cold was letting up somewhat. I didn't want to walk to the library today as I only walk there when I feel I really need a walk because again this is a bad neighborhood.

The library lately when I have been going hasn't been as busy and I found today that I would be able to get in quickly. I hadn't checked my hotmail account in a few days and so I pulled that up and found an interesting email there. The subject was something of relocation assistance please reply. When I pulled it up I figured it would be another one of those spam type deals but much to my pleasant surprise I found it to be from a real organization back in Ann Arbor. After reading it I almost shit my pants, it was from an agency saying that when I left in August my old apartment complex was forcing us all out due to providing it for lower income people and that I may qualify for a relocation check. Now let me bring you all up to speed, that was true the apartment complex that I was renting from was having all tenants in that building to move by I think October of 2008 because they were renovating it for some low income housing. Now I had my lease end in August and I figured that I could not be remotely in the running for this type of assistance.

Nevertheless, I needed cash big time and I thought that if I might just might be lucky enough to get something that would help with a move. So I clicked reply and sent the lady a message saying just that and waited to see what might happen. Having that out of the way I went on to Craigslist to search for some possible rooms that might be available. I first checked Ann Arbor and found a lot of listings but mostly sub let the deals which I didn't want to do. I didn't want to move back there and then after two or three months have to find other accommodations. So I posted my own ad saying that I would be looking in May or the middle part of that month and waited to see about that as well. The Milwaukee area was a bit tougher for me because I still didn't really know the city all that well and wasn't too strong on staying. I felt that I was starting to seriously consider moving back to Ann Arbor. Even though the economy is horrible there and the rent is still pretty expensive I knew people in the area like Kevin.

The next thing on my agenda while at the library was to search online and see if there might be some openings back in Ann Arbor. I wasn't too surprised at what came up and figured that if I did choose to go back that I would just use a staffing agency there and hopefully have better luck than I did here. My time on the computer was coming up and I was pretty beat and wanted to head back home and have a few beers and smokes and just watch some television and relax. Heading out I got hit up by yet another bum wanting some change or a cigarette, and I was like if I go back to Ann Arbor I won't have to experience much of that shit anymore. When I got back to the dump I started to think of that relocation assistance message I got and how it seemed to come at a time when I was at a sort of a crossroads. Now I am not too big on believing that it happened for a reason or any garbage like that I just found it to be interesting.

I started to wonder like many people do when thinking of what they would do if they were to come into some money.

Granted this wasn't the lottery but in some ways it was for me as the email said I might qualify for eleven hundred dollars! I grabbed my beer and smokes and turned on the music channel and sat on the floor. I really had some decisions to make coming up here in the next few months and this cash if I get it would make moving back to Ann Arbor not even a question. The money would also make the move so much simpler because I wouldn't be so tight for cash for awhile. That beer and smoke tasted mighty fine this day and my hopes were slightly lifted. My Zen moment was interrupted by Bobby who I could hear in the other room blasting his music. It doesn't take Bobby long either to change his mind and I guess rest got put in the back seat to a few cold ones I smiled and just shook my head in amazement.

The next day with great anticipation I wanted to get back to the library to see if I had received a response from the lady at the agency regarding my relocation assistance. Jumping in my car with great zest and squealing out of there like a bat out of hell I made the four block commute in three seconds it seemed to me. I soon noticed people standing outside and remembered that the library didn't open till one. Yes I know it stinks the library opens really late at this location. Getting my place in line I figured that it must be something that I can be approved for otherwise they would not have notified me. I mean many of these governmental agencies have to by law let those that might qualify know or suffer some sort of penalty I imagine. Finally the doors swing open and we all rush in to do whatever it is that we all needed to do. I get a computer and type my account number in a bit shaky because of the nerves and excitement. I pull up my hotmail account and see I did get a response from the lady.

Eagerly I open the message and begin to read and then it hits me that I am still eligible for this assistance! Furthermore, the response states that she had attached several forms for me to fill out and in detail told me where I needed to initial and where to sign. I almost shit a total and complete healthy one at that moment. She also said if I had any questions that I should contact her at the number she provided in her email signature. I had a few dollars on me and instantly put it on my card so I could print of these documents. I was a bit confused at the documents and being that I might be able to get eleven hundred dollars I didn't want to screw anything up. I knew that I would be calling her as soon as I got home. Man alive what a godsend although I had to still be a little guarded because I didn't actually have the check in hand. These things can take awhile and I knew that the sooner I got on top of this the sooner I would know whether I will actually get the money or be let down yet again.

Racing feverishly back to the dump with pages in hand I almost broke the door down trying to get in. Soon as I went to make the call I noticed the tell tale sound of that beeping noise, my phone was dying! I made sure before I made the call too that I had my charger and the appropriate paper and writing utensil handy. Dialing this angel I was so excited and she picked up quickly no voicemail thank god. I told her that I received her email about the relocation assistance and that I had some questions regarding the forms. She was very helpful and even remembered my email the other day which made me feel that she might actually be able to give me some personal attention in getting this matter done right and quickly. We went through the forms and she nicely told me where all the appropriate signatures and initials were to be placed and I did that while I had her on the line. I graciously said thank you and then asked her about my chances at getting this money. She laughed and said sweetie you get those forms to me before the deadline and I will send you a check.

My heart pounding with tears brimming to my eyes the first real good news I had heard in a long time and I was almost speechless. I told her that I would be taking care of all this today and told her if once she receives the paperwork if there is anything wrong to call me or email me. I then remembered to ask her if I get this to her in three days and all paperwork is good how long this might take till she can send me a check. She said about ten days after the receipt of all proper paperwork I will get the check so she said the first part of April or more like the tenth I should see it. Again with a hearty thank you I was off to the post office to send this out and get this check as soon as possible. With this new found information at hand I really started to think about moving back to Ann Arbor as a reality.

Folding the paperwork up and making sure I signed where I needed to and made sure all dates were right I headed to the post office on Martin Luther King Jr Boulevard just a few blocks from my dump. Pulling up to the post office I was again hit up by a bum for some spare change and I was now really feeling like I wanted to get the hell out of this place. I wanted to make sure that the lady at the agency would receive my paperwork as soon as possible so I sent it all next day priority. Now all there was to do was wait it out and see if indeed I would be receiving this money in the coming weeks. Heading back to the dump I got a call from Kevin L. and excitedly told him about the news. He was ecstatic too for me and asked then if I would be making my homecoming back to Ann Arbor or if I would be moving somewhere else here in Milwaukee. I didn't want to say anything for sure as I still didn't know; I mean it was coming down to basically this money.

If I receive this cash then I would be coming more than likely back to Ann Arbor, but if I didn't I was going to more than likely have to find another place here. After eight months though of being accosted by bums at every turn it seemed in the area I was living I was ready to get the hell out of here. Kevin was telling me not to worry and that things would work out that the money was mine it was just a matter of procedural shit until it came. I really needed that type of positive reinforcement. Anyway as I drove back I continued to talk to him about how nice it would be to live in a civilized environment again. I guess I never really knew what effect poverty and real poverty had on me as well as those in the community it affected most. The fear too that I felt being the only white person within miles of this place and feeling vulnerable not only economically but also physically really bothered me as well.

Arriving at my place I sat outside and talked with Kevin L. about my time frame for this move if the money should come by at the latest mid April. He asked me if I had any places lined up or any I was looking at through Craigslist. I told him I did look and I saw a few places but nothing that seemed to great right of hand. I also noted that I would probably find more luck in May because all the kids would be going home for summer and there should be a multitude of landlords wanting to fill rooms then. He seemed to agree and I basically said for the next ten days I will still apply around here for jobs if I see something but I am now in somewhat of a holding pattern. Kevin went on to talk about his plans of still moving out of the country and saying that he was really hoping something would work out there but wasn't holding his breath for it. I agreed somewhat but I was looking forward to seeing him again should he still be there in May if I came back. It is not often that you find a good friend that you can really talk honestly with about every type of subject imaginable.

I started to get cold outside and told Kevin that I would be in touch in the next few days and told him if he had anything that came up to call me as well. I felt pretty productive today after getting all these forms sent out and in a timely manner. I still had this nagging little voice in my head however that was telling me that it cannot possibly be this easy that no money is free and that more than likely something will come up that will be bad. I think that little voice was a good thing though I shouldn't be counting my chickens before they hatch and should be cautiously optimistic. I did want to tell everyone I could and I figured I could mention this development to my mother and see what she thinks about the moving possibility as well. I got a hold of my mom and told her that I might be able to get this assistance. She seemed pretty excited I mean who wouldn't be right eleven hundred dollars that you weren't expecting is never a bad thing.

I also wanted to tell her that I was considering moving back to Ann Arbor and that I missed my friends and the civility there. I think she was relieved a bit by this news as I was living in a shitty part of Milwaukee and it was a dangerous area. I wanted to maintain my sense of still not making any for sure plans as I didn't have any. I just told her the truth that I was waiting on this money and that I was sick of living here and that I was seriously looking at going back to Ann Arbor in May sometime. After that call I went over to Bobby's room because I wanted to tell him of this great news. Bobby was there and just having a few cold ones as he calls them. I told him I might get this money and Bobby seemed to be genuinely happy for me. He asked when I might know if I get it or not. I told him and asked him not to mention it to anyone especially our landlady. The last thing I would need is for her to start asking questions let alone start showing my place before I have other arrangements and he agreed to keep it quiet.

CHAPTER FOURTEEN

I started to reflect a bit while sitting there with Bobby having a beer about how time went so fast these last eight months. It truly is amazing how it slips by you even when you want it to it seems sad when you realize that it did. Bobby interrupted my deep thought with the question of my cable and if I was still having problems with it. Shaking my head a bit to get out of my daze I said no I was getting a great reception as of late. It seemed he was having problems with his but since I have been there I noticed that Bobby doesn't know much at all about the television and the cable setup. A few times over the course that I have been here I have helped him with it. He would always say it isn't working and all that and most the time Bobby either unplugged it or it wasn't even plugged in or he didn't know how to turn the power on through the remote. Of course this was very humorous to me but I didn't want to let him know that in case it might cause him some embarrassment. I would often figit around it and make it look like I was doing something and then say there it goes its working.

Bobby was always very appreciative and was like man I don't know this thing is a piece of junk. It made me laugh and I felt that was more than enough of payment for me. We sat there for most the afternoon just drinking some beers and watching some investigative crime show. It was nice I was in an optimistic mood and I really wanted to just sit here and enjoy myself with Bobby today. I didn't know how many more days like this we might have and I had grown to like Bobby quite a bit. It was funny I turned around and looked in the kitchen and there was Bobby's oven left on and open as to get more heat in this dump. The landlady did seem to be making it work better but I think Bobby just liked it a bit warmer than she had it set at. It reminded me of the times earlier in the year where we both had our ovens open trying to get whatever little eat we could out of them. This is a tough life he has led and was rough on me too. Poverty is a total bitch and is something that can rob a man of not only his pride but his soul.

I asked him about the oven and said was he still not getting any heat up in there. Bobby said it seemed to him that it turned on once in a while but it never was really consistent. I knew that wasn't true on my side so I checked his vents thinking that in a drunken type stupor Bobby might have shut them and then forgot he did. Upon inspection I could see they were all open and I asked if he mentioned anything to our landlady. Bobby was pretty fed up and said I am tired of complaining about shit to her it is more work than just taking it. I could totally understand that remark because she was pretty slow on the up take but she did try to make the problems better when told about them. I knew after Bobby told me about his problem that I would have to tell her instead. I thought that many landlords must be doing this to their tenants. Taking advantage of the disadvantaged and poor people playing on their apathy and poverty it pisses me off royal. After most the afternoon and night went by I told Bobby to take care and that we would have to get together again tomorrow or sometime soon and I retired for the day.

It was April first today April fools day and I wanted to go check my P.O. Box downtown to see if by chance I received the check and if not I wanted to go work out at Bally's and then hit the library because she might have sent an email to me. Yes I almost forgot, about a month ago I believe it was the first week in March that I did get a Bally's membership at the downtown location. I wanted to start working out once in awhile and try to get in better shape. Now I have never been the gym going type but I figured if I spend some money on it I will go often. Well that hasn't been the case this last month as I only went twice and I was feeling like I was throwing what little money I had totally away. The first time I went I actually hit the bikes and rode for about thirty minutes and then I went for a soak in the hot tub and a steam after that. I was trying to take better care of myself a bit I guess although every time I try to it always is a miserable attempt. And the second time all I did was hit the hot tub again. I guess in part because it was cold in my place somewhat and I wanted to warm up a bit.

Today was going to be a different day I was going to run these errands and get my money's worth and hit the bikes again. Also the optimism over my possible new found fortune that might be coming gave me some extra wind in my sails. I also had the ware with all to get a national plan so that if I moved I can use it anywhere in the country where there's a Bally's. Pretty smart because if I do move back to Ann Arbor there is a Bally's there so I could just use that club. Now it actually has only been around a week since I sent that paperwork back to the lady in Ann Arbor but I figured I was going to be down in that area anyway so why not check the box and perhaps maybe it will be there. It was a nice day out today as well and the sun was melting a bit of the snow letting water stream in the parking lot. It all seemed to be looking rosy for me and I wasn't going to lose that thought today. Like I have said earlier, when you get the gift of positive feelings and optimism try to hold on to it for dear life as pain and disappointment are just around the corner waiting to take over.

There was no check in my box only more of the same, bills. So off to the gym I headed still feeling like a few bucks. The gym is interesting to me as everyone in there seems to have all the appropriate knowledge of the clothing that is worn and also of the etiquette. This being my third time in a month and maybe not too many more overall I was a bit nervous as how to carry myself.

What did I care right I had the duffle bag the shorts and tennis shoes and towel all that I needed. I went for the bikes, I like them it isn't all too difficult on you and it is a good place I think to start when trying to get back into some kind of shape. Everyone else around me however was like they were training for the Tour de France I mean my god these people were crazy. Sweat flying off them and then drinking furiously out of their water bottles to rehydrate it was really weird. Now I have never been one of these types of nut jobs and to be honest I never will be and I am glad by that revelation. I am just not that into myself I guess and do not dedicate a lot of time and energy let alone money on self preservation or self glorification.

The workout went well for me I lasted another thirty minutes on the bike and felt that I had done well. After that I headed back into the locker room and saw a wall of men's asses and penises presented before me. Some old, some young, some fat, some skinny a total array of naked men. Yeah I was like well when in Rome right. So I do I bared all and strutted around like a peacock and had a nice shower. It is tough to have a good shower when you have so many people around but I figured this shower couldn't be any worse than the one I used at home. I felt that at least I got some of my money's worth through this workout and headed back to the ghetto to check my email at the library. Driving back from downtown and heading back into the north side I saw the total difference between the two it was quite striking.

I was a bit nervous as to what I might find when I open up my email today I am really hoping that the little negative voice that was telling me this is too good to be true would not be found to be correct. I had no time to be hesitant and not check it as if there was something wrong and that needed to be corrected I wanted to know immediately. Punching in my email address nervously and password I clicked and waited to see if I had anything new in my inbox. There were six messages in black bold text next to my inbox icon. Taking a deep breath in and then slowly exhaling it out I clicked with my eyes shut. Opening them slowly I saw that indeed there was a message from the lady at the agency. Dammit I thought, shit this is more than likely going to be a note saying I didn't qualify or something I just knew it. You cannot know Lee unless you open it I said to myself and when I started to read it I was relieved. The message was saying that I just messed up on copying my driver's license and a few of the initials. My god what a relief so I was going to print it all out again and recopy my driver's license again and see what she says on the phone.

As I got her on the phone I asked if I could just fax it all over to her so she can start up on it again more quickly. Unfortunately that would not work the actual pen marks needed to be seen and also with my initials next to the corrections that I had to make. Still it wasn't a total denial of the funds and I took it as I am still in this thing and that I might actually get this money. Off I ran again back to the post office to next day this all out again. This was starting to get expensive, well not expensive in most peoples standards however I am on a super tight budget and seven dollars here and there starts to add up. After running all these errands and working out I was pretty beat. My anxiety was still high as I really just wanted to know if I was going to get the money or if I wasn't. I called Kevin L. soon as I got back to my dump and told him that some of the paperwork was filled out wrong I guess and that she needed me to resend some information back.

Kevin L. didn't seem too worried by this development which didn't make me feel reassured. I told him that it is too good to be true that more than likely something would come up and I would be screwed. Time he said is a bitch but sometimes all we have is that and to go and grab a beer or two and chill out. He didn't have to tell me to grab a few beers shit I had one open by that time already. Kevin said that if needed he can always go down and ask for me, but I said that wasn't going to be necessary and to just wait like he said. I have never been the one to be the patient type I guess, but I should be better at it considering I have had to wait on a lot this last year. I told him I needed to get off the phone and just be by myself right now and that I hoped to god this cash comes through.

The next few days went by a bit slower than usual as I was thinking about how nice it would be to get the hell out this shithole. On the other hand I new that when I got back to Ann Arbor it would not be an easy go of it for me either. I knew that the job market there was pretty piss poor and had to make my mind up as to why I was really going to return there if in fact this money came through. I basically came up with the notion that I would not be going back there for the job market because that would be a totally garbage argument to make. I decided that there were in part two reasons that I would be returning to that area. The first reason was that I knew people back there. Granted I didn't know all too many people but a few and they were good friends to me most of the time. I really in the last few years of my life have found it to be terribly difficult to meet new people that could end up becoming a good confidant and friend. I mean the story goes in America that you meet your wife in college and then that is your life you work your ass off to keep her happy and spit out a few kids.

Well that didn't happen for me shit it didn't even come remotely close as far as I can remember. I mean I met Kevin L. at one of my jobs and a few others and that's it basically. Or sometimes I suppose you meet your neighbors and they can become a good source of friendship as well. For me though I found it pretty hard to have people that would come into my life that were agreeable to my high standards I guess in some way. I had a few people tell me when discussing women that I just had to high of standards and that's why I was single. My rebuttal to that is they should take a look at some of them that I did date and they would see that was totally not true. In serious analysis however I do concede the fact that I may expect a lot out of people that I let into my weird little world. I am not easily impressed by dumb conversations and very shallow people with not to much to say. I find many people that I encounter to be rather dull and totally typical very cookie cutter as I would say.

I did know that when I go back assuming all goes well here with the money and that I don't get mugged I will at least have some support. I think that is vital for me these days that I cannot just sit in this dump surrounded by people who never had a life and are never going to strive for one. The apathy that is surrounding me here in Milwaukee is pretty suffocating. I do have empathy for a lot of these people I don't want to use the word pity because I believe that word to be terribly condescending. A lot of them were dead as soon as they were born in a lot of ways and they are doing the best that they can. So I know that I do have some education behind me and staying here is a total waste of my time right now and to head back to a community and people that can actually stimulate my mind a bit.

Even in Ann Arbor it was hard for me to find new and lasting worthwhile relationships. I mean what do you do go up to someone you might have a mere acquaintance with and say hey you wanna be friends like in grammar school? I have tried with some women here to do just that well not that actually ask them out and I get the look of who the hell are you to be talking to me look. Maybe like many people have said that when it happens it happens. I suppose that's right although as more time goes by and I get a bit more hardened it is going to be more difficult for me to open up and allow such a relationship to transpire.

The second reason for going back that I came up with was the fact that I simply didn't feel very safe in my current surroundings. Now I must admit since coming here eight months ago my car has never been broken into and I haven't been mugged. But the sense of tension that pervaded the area was tangible and real. Especially perhaps for myself seeing that I was the only white man around these parts that actually lived here. I mean the few times I would go to the corner liquor store on seventh and Locust I received many looks of suspicion and rage. That is why I drove my car often even to the library many times which was only four blocks away because I didn't feel comfortable. Like I have said before the depression that is palatable here has been adding I believe in some way to my own sense of self. Looking around everyday at filth and the walking dead isn't very pleasant or uplifting.

I think back about a town next to Ann Arbor called Ypsilanti that I have often heard be referred to as the hood by a lot of people in Ann Arbor. I laugh now when I think of people considering that city a bad part of town or a bad place to live. I mean north side Milwaukee is bad and dangerous shit I have heard my share of gunshots going off around here. Experience is everything I truly believe that. You cannot really know what is what unless you honestly lived it through and through. I mean many people like I am sure I have said before can say they understand your situation and could put themselves into your shoes, but to put it simply they cannot truly grasp the immensity of poverty if they haven't been truly hungry. I hope that no more people continue to be hungry and live in total destitution, but it still will no matter how badly I want it to not be the reality for them. I have learned from a lot I have seen here and let me tell you it sticks with you.

So I believe that by being back in Ann Arbor which is a very safe city that I will be able to clear my stress load as far as the tension that this place creates. I started to think how black men have a problem with hyper tension and no wonder this shit is stressful just being, let alone being harassed by police or worrying about getting shot, just sitting around can be stressful. Hopefully I can relax if I can go back to Ann Arbor and not worry about walking the streets after dark or shit in the daytime. Hopefully I will not have to see the filth that litters the streets and yards around me. I mean Ann Arbor compared to this place that I have been living at is like fucken Disneyland man. I would have never known that this was a very nice city if I never had left and lived in a more undesirable place. It's like that song from the rock group Cinderella, "you don't know what you got till it's gone." I liken that also to my sense of losing my hope and optimism as well and find it to be an appropriate song in many situations.

I need to today go to the library and check on my email and also the P.O. Box that I have and see if there is any word on the check. I hate waiting it drives me nuts having to be on someone else's time frame or work ethic. Anyway I think that those two reasons are perfectly appropriate reasons for moving back and I feel that I have given this city eight months and applied to everything imaginable and have gotten zero in return. It is now the first week of April and the lady told me either this week or the middle of the month so I am really chomping at the bit for something soon. As I am driving to downtown I ask myself if I really did make a decent go of Milwaukee or if I am just running back to what is familiar. I really questioned myself because I hate to make any decision in haste especially of this magnitude. The conclusion that I came to is that I did! I mean the area I am living in wasn't the sole reason for moving back. And I suppose I could move to a better part of town here in Milwaukee although I am sure it would not be as cheap as what I am paying now.

No, I was applying to jobs in all the parts of the city and surrounding suburbs and was not getting anything. I did make a good effort out of it and am comfortable with my decision to move back. Pulling into the store I went in and was hoping to see that envelope there waiting for me. It did not happen this day but I knew that I had still a cushion of time until I would start to get really worried. Yes, this has been the bulk of many of my days lately not to eventful just doing the same few things day after day. I wanted to make sure I didn't receive an email from the lady so I managed to check my email as well and found nothing there from her.

With no new information at hand I managed to think of a great time killer. I needed in a major way to start cleaning my place up not only in case I do move but because it needed it. Keeping ones mind occupied in times of stress can be difficult that is for sure. Looking around my place as soon as I got back I could easily tell that there wasn't enough filth to keep me busy for that long. I managed to do what clean up that needed to be done however I felt this nagging feeling to go back to the library and see if I might be able to find any rooms online in Ann Arbor. This managing of my time is like a full time job I swear I mean I am trying to be productive and upbeat but time has a way of making you feel like you are merely treading water. Screw it I said as I took control of myself and grabbed my keys and headed back to the library in the hopes of some good rooms to rent. In Ann Arbor rooms for rent are not hard to come by, but it is hard to find a good room that is available, and even harder to have good roommates.

When I arrived there I was in the mindset of a typically bored person tying to kill some time. When I got there I was reminded by one of the attendants to shut my phone off. It is funny considering all the other people seem to take calls when they are in the computer area, but I suppose I was an oddity and therefore she noticed my presence. Sitting there and trying to look online for something my boredom was becoming overwhelming. Listening to the clack and click of the keys that others were pressing on and the hip hop music blaring through their headphones I felt pretty enraged. I just wanted to know and know now. I managed to check email and go online to check for a few jobs but found nothing worth talking about. I did however find a nice location at a few rooms in Ann Arbor close to one of my friends. The amount of rent was the same I was paying here at this dump so I figured that it might not be a bad idea to give this one guy a call.

The location of this room was only four blocks away from one of my previous residences and also my friend. I dialed the number and hoped that the room would be available next month considering also if I do manage to even get this check. The man on the other line seemed very kind and nice and stated that the room was actually being used at this moment however it would be becoming vacant in May. What perfect timing I thought to myself I mean it was like someone was saying to me get the fuck out of dodge. I let him know that I was in Milwaukee and planning to move back to the area soon and he just said keep in touch but I cannot make any promises. I too in turn made basically the same response as I didn't even know what was going to happen with my future as I was on perma hold waiting for that check or the news that I wasn't going to get it. I felt pretty confident that if I did so choose to go back that I would have no problem finding appropriate lodging. I took the number as well of a few different places that I saw when I was searching but nothing was as close to the area I found earlier. I figured that when I got back to my place I would call the lady at the agency and ask her if there were any new developments considering my case.

Killing time can be hard I started to think about how easy it is when you get majorly intoxicated because I found that to be a great way of accomplishing that. I didn't want to be that way and wanted to be in the present especially considering this new development with this check. I called the agency and got a hold of the lady and much to my excitement and great pleasure she told me that she was sending the check out the next day. Some great news to put it lightly I was astounded and took a double take as I asked her to repeat herself to make sure I was not dreaming. She just laughed it off in her polite sounding voice and said yes it will be sent through certified mail out tomorrow and you should get it in a few days. She wanted to make sure the address was correct before she sent it and told me she was going to call me that day anyway to confirm this information. With everything confirmed and me now knowing I was getting a check I felt like a marathon runner at mile twenty five.

I was hoping that the finish would come but was not willing to take anything for granted. I wanted to jump for joy and scream aloud at this great news I mean it is not often that you get told you are going to receive an eleven hundred dollar check for basically nothing. I had to call Kevin L. right away and when I got a hold of him I think he new that this call was going to be a good one not a bad miserable diatribe of shame and depression. I told him that in a few days hopefully I should have the check and that I would be moving back sometime in May. He too seemed pretty ecstatic and was telling me I told you so and things of that nature. I was telling him how earlier that day I found a place close to where I once lived and that it was the same amount that I am paying here. He laughed it off and said hey man at least back here you won't have to worry about being accosted. I laughed as I agreed and thanked him for all his positive reinforcement lately because I really needed it.

I called the landlord I spoke with earlier after getting off the phone with Kevin L. and told him I was more than likely now at this point to come back. He again said that is wonderful however he could not reserve the place for me as that was not his policy. I understood I wish I had the money and a place lined up now because I would be so gone at this point. Now it was a serious time wait position I was in. I felt like I could here the tick and tock of the clock waiting ever so patiently and yet trembling inside. There was really nothing I could do at this moment besides just waiting. I grabbed a few beers and went out on my porch watching the degenerates stumble on by. Having a few cold ones is never a bad thing lately for me and the entertainment that can be seen around here for free is totally priceless. My mind wondering off into some dream I wanted the seconds, minutes, and hours to just fly by quickly.

Sitting there I felt a great sense of actually knowing that I did what I needed to do here and that my sentence so to speak was over. What I mean by my sentence is that it truly has felt the whole time that I have been here like I was in some kind of real prison. Looking around the neighborhood I new that I was definitely ready to move out of here and that maybe just maybe Ann Arbor might be able to give me what I need this time around. Of course that little voice in my head kept plotting against any thoughts of optimism and was telling me not to count on anything until it was happening right in front of me. I suppose that is a good aspect of life to have that gnawing self doubt to some extent always keeping you one your toes and not taking anything for granted. On the other hand this gnawing voice makes it hard to appreciate and enjoy the good times that might be at hand. I just knew that I needed to keep my mind off of this all and try to get my gear together and prepare myself for the fact that I might be getting out of here soon and to not watch the clock so hard.

I had lined up a few other temporary rooms for rent in Ann Arbor as well as I wanted to have something to go back to instead of having to rely on a friends couch. The rooms were just that rooms and for the same price and I knew that by leaving I would be giving up the luxury of having my own kitchen space. That has been truly nice to have here and I am not looking forward to sharing a fridge with a bunch of others because I have found that food disappears quite easily in those living situations. Nevertheless, I started to some cleaning up and getting most of my gear together. It was mid April now and I knew that any day that check should be in my box. I fought over when I should tell my landlady that I would be bouncing out of here. I figured I would tell her as soon as I got the check because if I told her and then didn't receive the check I might be ass out on the street regardless.

This afternoon I figured it should be here and knew that certified mail comes pretty quickly. It was starting to feel very surreal as I stood in this place I couldn't believe I went through all this and been here almost nine months already. I still was a bit nervous about returning to Ann Arbor as well as lately any decision that I make is merely on pure speculation. I have had a few people ask me why I think it will be better back in Michigan and my only response is at least I will not be in harms way or have a high potential for it to come my way. In this economy and with the absolute decay of America as a whole I think unless you have some serious connections and inside trading so to speak we are all merely floating around with any decision we make. At least that's how I feel over the course of the last year anyhow.

The day hopefully of truth was to come and I grabbed my coat and keys and headed to downtown Milwaukee to check my box. As I drove down that song that goes, time, time, tickin, tickin, tickin away, was playing and I just smiled and said how appropriate. As I pulled into the parking lot I couldn't hesitate one more minute and basically ran into the office and saw a parcel waiting for me to open. With key inserted and a brisk turn to the right I reached in with my left hand and pulled out a certified letter! Still not believing my great luck here I ravaged the container that was holding my parole ticket if you will and saw a beautiful check with eleven hundred dollars on it and payable to me! Fuck yeah I said aloud and I am sure I grabbed the attention of the workers there but fuck it man this was freedom of sorts. Skipping back to my car like a schoolgirl in puppy love I headed to my bank with the urgency of now as Obama says. The one thing that was rattling my mind as I pulled into the bank was that the address on my driver's license and account was not accurate to the address that was on the check.

Meaning that I was worried that one of the twelve year old high school drop out tellers would be giving me some kind of shit. Then I remembered that this was a branch that was run by mainly black women. Now sometimes the stereotype of them is true as sassy and terribly bitchy however these ones could careless if I was passing a check in the name of Ronald Reagan. Ease came into me and I approached the thick huge glass partition that was there and slid my checking deposit slip and check over with a smile and started to do some conversating. She was a cute little thing very ripe for the picking and after a few seconds handed me back my slip and I looked at the deposit and account to make sure she didn't fuck anything up and then was at total peace. The deposit was great and everything went through I had over twelve hundred in my account and I was ready to call my landlady and tell her that I would be leaving in a few weeks. I still had this month paid for and I didn't feel a great need to waste that money either by leaving early plus it would give me more time to room search and job search a bit too.

I headed to the liquor section of a store nearby and got me some cold ones as Bobby would say to celebrate. Heading back to the hood I knew that I didn't have to be here much longer and that hopefully very soon things would be much better. Once I pulled in I grabbed my phone and dialed my landlady's number. I told her that I would be moving out by the fist of may, and that I might be moving a few days earlier than the first or a few days later providing I have a room back in Ann Arbor or not. She seemed a bit surprised and a bit annoyed that I would be leaving. I told her that I wanted tot give her a decent notice so she could put a ad up in a week or so. Little did I know the terrible annoyance that would be deposed on me in the next coming days. She said she wished me well and hoped that I might be able to find what I am looking for back in Michigan. I went and told Bobby about the news and wanted to slam some cold ones with him to celebrate today.

Bobby was pretty happy for me it seemed and of course the free beers never hurt him being in a good mood for you. He was asking as to how much longer I would be staying here and I told him a few more weeks and that I would be gone back to Michigan. Man you have to do what you have to do Bobby said. I told him to that this wasn't the appropriate area for a white boy to be kicking it at anyway. Bobby really agreed and said yeah man this area isn't meant for you and that I should have always left here and even earlier in his opinion. You know many say we need to all get along and live together and my only response is that yes that might be able to be done if there is a true mixture of cultures and races, but one white boy and blocks of blacks doesn't do that to well. Although I learned a lot about what goes on in these types of neighborhoods and the characters that are created here. Bobby started to laugh and go you crazy nigga man Lee I tell you man now lets drink a few of these cold ones before they get warm.

The first of May is now here and the last several days have been very exciting as well as very annoying. My landlady didn't waste much time in posting the ad which I suppose is fine the only thing that is annoying to me is that she expects me to have everything perfectly cleaned while she goes on vacations. What I mean by that is I told her she can keep my security deposit because I would have to stay here a few more days and I didn't think that was fair. I figured letting her have the deposit for allowing me a few more days to stay was more than ample compensation not only for the few extra days here in May but also for the cleaning that she felt might not be up to her standards. I have to confess I mean I am not a great cleaner however the apartment is in almost the same state of cleanliness that it was when I moved in nine months ago. She has been stopping over quite a bit and that too has been annoying me. I just wish once these slum lords would let you actually move out until they start showing up with new degenerates to move in. Now I know most apartment complexes do similar things it's just that it annoys the shit out of me.

Anyway she seemed fine with that arrangement and wanted confirmation that I would be out in a few days. I told her I would be and that she had no need to worry about anything. When I asked her if she was going to be here to collect my keys she told me that she would be going on yet another vacation and that I could just put them in an envelope for her. This was another thing that bothered me with this situation. I mean here I am along with the others that reside here and we are barely getting by, yet she collects are cash and goes on vacation after vacation, it must be nice. I guess when you are poor, hungry, unemployed, and in general pissed off at your circumstance it doesn't really help to have a landlord that basically flaunts it in your face that you are paying for their repeated vacations.

Moving on I needed to go back to the library on King Boulevard to make sure that I had indeed pretty much confirmed a new dump to live in. I found this other place that was around three blocks from where I once lived too. One of my friends that I met when living there was my next door neighbor and I was pretty much hoping that I could secure this place. Now there were no pictures of the room which is always a bit troubling but I figured that being in that area which was a nice area that I need not worry about it. Contacting this landlord he seemed very pleasant and eager to confirm that I would be coming in the next few days. The rent was exactly what I was paying here the only thing that sort of stood out was that there were five others living in the house at the time. I told him that I would want the room and said that I would call him once I arrived back in town.

There were a few others I had seen that looked promising but I figured that this place couldn't be all that bad. Once being reassured that the room would be mine and held by him I felt like I was not just going home with no home that at least I would have a place to go back to. I called my parents to let them in on the fact that I would be indeed returning back to the Ann Arbor area and they seemed to be neither overly joyed nor overly cynical. That was nice not that their actual opinion regarding this matter would have any real impact on my decision it was just nice not to get some line. You know the line of you were there before and the market and all that sucked then what's going to make it any better now that type of rebuttal. I also wanted to contact a few of my friends back home too and let them know not only because I figured they would be happy with my decision but also just in case I needed to crash a night or two at their place in the event that this landlord didn't show up when he agreed to. They were pretty excited about the news and said that they hoped it would yield some better results than some of my previous experiences.

That night I can remember talking to one of my friends who at the time was living in Chicago. He moved too from Ann Arbor shortly after I moved to Milwaukee because he lost his job back there and wanted also to give a bigger city a try. He kept giving me the saying that the market in Michigan is awful and that you are going to have a tough time back there finding anything. Like I said earlier in this book when I was pondering what reasons I would be giving for this move if I was to do it was not for a job but more for security and familiarity. Of course, he said but I just think you should think about how hard this is going to be there for you again. He stated for the thousandth time that the cost of living there is a lot comparable to the wages one gets paid and how was I going to manage that. All the things he said were true yet falling on totally deaf ears at this point. I mean I have been in a pretty large city here in Milwaukee for nine damn months and really had only two relevant interviews. I think no matter where I went in this country with my experience and education level that I would be in a world of shit either way.

This is why I hate telling people my decisions or thoughts on many things because there doesn't seem to be anybody that can just say hey man good luck kick ass and keep in touch. It really irritates me because when they give their half ass script rebuttals they are assuming that I haven't already gone through these questions. I don't know sometimes I wish I didn't know anyone so I wouldn't have to here their reasons of disapproval or condescending comments. I would like to think that I am pretty supportive of my friends and family and try not to be the judge and jury and then the executioner. Like the saying goes however, we are all human, and I need to sometimes just take certain thoughts from others with a grain of salt.

With the people that matter most to me knowing that I indeed would be making a return of total defeat I felt a little bit better that most were supportive and understanding. I think if those people that were on the fence could see how it has been here for me the last nine months that they would be jumping for joy at this news. Unfortunately no eyes have the gift of seeing others we care about when at a distance so I must not be dwelling on others right now and concentrating on my own plans. I figured I would be leaving in a few days and that it wouldn't take too much to get my gear into my little Saturn car, maybe just an hour or two. With that I wanted to tell the store that I had my P.O. Box at that I would be moving and ask them when I knew my actual address if they could forward any mail that would be left.

I figured I would do that tomorrow as it was evening now and the store would be more than likely closed.

I started to do a lot of reflecting on how this all seemed like a total waste of my time and how I did in a small way feel like I failed. It just sucks when you make a move and think that you are going to have something better come along and then nothing does. In fact, I almost feel at times with my life that I am moving backwards and not forwards. This economy has really kicked the shit out of me and I often wonder when I will be able to have a decent job again. When I say decent I mean making maybe fifteen dollars an hour which is shit money in any reasonably sized city these days. This last year now has been a pile of total shit and I often wonder if it indeed is truly over here for not only me but us as Americans. I guess sometimes its better not to think about things that are so out of hand and just concentrate on the fact that I have twelve hundred dollars in my account and I will be moving back to an area that is safer and familiar.

I went into my bedroom slash living room part of the dump and turned on the television to the music channels. I also needed to grab a few cold ones too as the reminiscing was definitely going to be going down tonight. When I sat back down with my usual beer and smoke going accompanied with some soft rock I could hear that the neighborhood outside was starting to come out of its winter hibernation. Last summer when I came here back on the first of august it was pretty wild. A lot of people walking around, a lot of base being pumped through the litter ridden streets it was really amazing. I was so done with that though as I pulled hard on my beer and tried to relax. The ruckus and occasional gun shot that could be hard, along with the three a.m crack whore banging on my door looking for someone else was something I would always remember but was done with.

Now I am not going to say I was a poster boy the whole time I was here as I am sure you can tell from reading this. I mean I partied hard and did some stupid things as well. I am not a little schoolboy surrounded by all these savages; I too was becoming one or maybe was in a certain way all along. I just knew that if I stayed here and didn't get back to some sort of civilization that I would definitely be in a bad rut. At least back in Ann Arbor there are a lot more people there that seem to be educated and wanting to excel. Sitting here I was pretty proud of myself at the fact that I managed not to get hurt or get into any trouble while being here. I felt like I really knew now poverty and struggle and that this experience was not something that most people get. I mean most white college educated people, you know seeing it on a movie or hearing some rap lyrics. This shit is real and it is very sad in a lot of ways but there is a lot of potential, a shit load of potential too all around waiting to be awakened.

The beers now flowing well I figured that I needed to get most of my gear that I could near the door and start to do a bit of cleanup. I hate cleaning but it is always nice when you have a beer buzz and some music playing in the background. Cleaning this and that off the countertops and starting to see the room resemble the way it was when I moved in last August was weird. Sometimes when I move out of places and it is basically the same as it was when I first got here I feel like I need to ask myself a question. The question I often ask myself is, "was I really here calling this home?" I don't know it probably sounds terrifically stupid but I feel like am leaving a piece of me here as I go or am I taking a piece with me? Perhaps a little of both would be more accurate. With that I needed some sleep as I was getting even myself a bit worn out by all the deep thought.

The following morning my landlady was nice enough to stop by again and in tow she had a man that wanted to see the place. Luckily for me I had done some pretty good drunk cleaning the night before and she seemed to be appreciative. The guy looked pretty rough, a tall lanky black man with some worn out clothes on. I thought of Bobby and he might not get along too much and I actually worried about how that whole thing would be for him after I leave. I mean Bobby and I were a pretty darn good team and I looked after him and was worried that with his disability and drinking that someone might try to take advantage of him. With that thought going through my head I spoke up and told him that the other guy is really nice and that for the most part it is really respectful up in here. He pretty much looked at me with a look of who are you and whatever. Finally they left and I told the landlady that I would leave the key for him in the second mailbox in two days when I was leaving.

I heard Bobby up and around and wanted to tell him that I might have met his new housemate. Bobby was half drunk and was telling me he didn't care and that he better watch it. He was playing some of that old school music he likes and by now I have to tell you it grew on me a bit too. He asked me if I wanted one of his tapes that he uses in his beat up boom box. I was like no Bobby man I cannot do that man those are your tracks that you enjoy. Of course Bobby wasn't taking no for an answer and said that he would actually make me up a tape that day. I asked him for his phone number as I said that I would like to stay in touch and he was more than willing to do that. I started to get the feeling that I was going to cry for some odd reason. I mean it really started to hit me how we had actually become friends in a way. Many people have their own version of what they claim friendship to be to them and I am not sure Bobby would claim me but I sort of claimed him much to my surprise.

I was really getting close to welling up and I didn't want him to see that as I had to be a tough man. Then it hit me Bobby saw me cry before a few times and in a lot worse shape. Nevertheless I managed to keep it all together and we both said how nice it was to have each other living here. We both acknowledged how it could have been worse for both of us if we had some real thugs in the place. It was really nice to be having this sort of goodbye although I new later that night or perhaps tomorrow maybe Bobby would have that tape but I wasn't really wanting it nor expecting it. With that I left and tucked his number in my pants and went off to check my box one more time and to let them know I would be calling soon with my new address. They were cool about it at the box store and even though I still owed a month I told them I would call and pay that over the phone once settled back in Michigan.

I wanted to hit up the grocery store the Pic and Save that I always shopped at one more time to get some pasta and some brews. When I was checking out I saw this nice black woman that I always seemed to chit chat a bit with. She was always very pleasant and had a good hearty laugh when I would describe certain things that were going on in my life here. I told her I was getting out of dodge and that I was heading back to Ann Arbor. She was like oh why did it not work out good for you here? I was like you know the situation and told her I came into that check from the advocacy agency and was taking that money to start again. I was going to miss her a bit too I guess we hugged each other and after a brief talk said our goodbyes and good lucks. I wish I wasn't so damn sentimental, I mean here as I am leaving the store I am again feeling a bit sad. I guess what it says now that I can reflect a bit is the real fact of how few people I actually had conversations with while staying here in Milwaukee. It really hit me that I was basically for nine months on my own in a serious interpersonal way. That I had a few brief passing byes whether it be with Bobby for a few hours drinking, or the check out lady for ten minutes.

Driving back to the hood and leaving the downtown area I really was feeling down and out. I just stared ahead and drove with the radio in silence and my mind and body in a sort of limbo. It was like I was on automatic pilot the next thing I remember in a way is just sitting in the parking lot to the dump. Snapping out of it I told myself that even though you miss these people they really weren't longtime friends and for that matter I guess the store lady wasn't even a friend just an acquaintance. When I got back into the dump I wanted to start cleaning out the fridge and get that done as that would be pretty much the last thing to do. The landlady wanted me to use some serious elbow grease on the oven but I was like yeah okay whatever. The oven wasn't all that bad and I was sick and tired of doing anymore cleaning, as well as this new person probably would trash this place anyhow I felt.

I called Bobby back over as I had some herbs and some things that I figured he might be able to use. Bobby took it all as he never is one to waste anything that's for sure. That made me feel good that I could give him some stuff that I know he would use. After that Bobby said he was going to take a nap I believe and left, and again I said if we don't see each other take care man. I started to slam some cold ones back and went to sit back in the room. I knew that if I was going to leave tomorrow that I would have to get up pretty early as my landlady said to be out by noon. Now moving no matter how little is never fun when you are half in the bag hung over. So finally as the afternoon came around I started to move the gear I could into my trunk of my car. I was doing pretty well too and figured I might be able to get most of the packing done this afternoon. As I was putting things in the trunk I saw a few people watching what I was up to. This disturbed me a bit and I started to think that this was not a good idea to do and then leave it there overnight.

Then I started to get angry at the fact that on my last night would be the night of all nights that I would have some asshole or assholes break into my car. With rage and basic contempt for this shit anymore I made a command decision to move out that night. I rushed back into my place and started to deflate my shitty air mattress and grab all the rest of my gear and get at it. I got the rest into the back and front seats of my car and had that baby packed in thirty minutes it seemed. I did a quick look over of the room to make sure that I did not leave anything important. Feeling confident about that I did a quick sweep under and around where my air mattress was and then said it is done I'm out of here. I took the keys off and put them into an envelope and wrote good luck to the new person once I had locked the door and put the keys in the box. I wanted to wake Bobby up but knew he wouldn't answer more than likely and just said another day another time maybe one day.

I had some beers in the car also to aid in the drive back to Ann Arbor which would only take around four hours or so. I was ready to leave I just wanted to get back into Ann Arbor and even if I had to for the night I could get a hotel room and relax for a night. I got onto interstate forty three south and was on my way. With the Milwaukee's skyline passing to my left and rain clouds to my right I just sat back had a smoke and said goodbye, I tried, and hopefully this time I will succeed.

THE END

CONCLUSION

I first of all would like to thank all of you who read this story. This story was an important one for me to tell especially in this time of difficulty not only for myself but also for many others out there. When I first got to Milwaukee that August day in 2008 I was shocked at what I was going to call my new home. It was deplorable as far as my standards were at the time. I really thought to myself what the hell are you getting yourself into? I wasn't sure but knew I had no where else to go so of course I pushed on. It truly was a different world one that I never expected nor thought I would have to encounter.

I was in a pretty dark place a lot of the time over the course of this book and I saw it returned almost mirror imaged back to me by the people in the neighborhood. The amount of shear poverty and hopelessness was really suffocating. Like I said earlier I believe in the book about trying to help up a girl who fell on her bike in front of me and getting the coldest look. I knew then that this was not going to be an easy experience and just maybe a very dangerous one too. I really wanted people to feel the pain and suffering that I saw and also was going through.

I think that there are many like me who have been fighting so hard and for so very long. I wanted the reader to acknowledge some of the deep thoughts that they might have regarding certain topics that I brought up. I not only wanted the reader to feel the emotions of despair or sadness but also and more appropriately the feeling of anger. The feeling of impotence at the fact of not having a way to make a great deal of change as to your own personal situation.

I hope that the reader if in a position of wealth or power will lessen any idea of poor people just being lazy and being deserving of suffering. I hope that this will start a real dialogue in this country, and more importantly a dialogue in your homes with family and friends, and also your local communities. There is real suffering in this world. If you the reader have the means then help those around you that are in need.

If we call our country a compassionate country then let us act on our motto. I just hope lastly that you all enjoyed this novel and maybe it will make you think and at times cry. And just maybe it will make you be appreciative for what you do have instead of angry at what you don't have because there are many that have nothing and never will have anything.

Thank you,

Lee K. Sanford

Thank you to the following:

Ann Arbor District Library
Bobby B.
Brad B.
Kevin L.
Milwaukee Public Library
Raj
Roger L.

Printed in the United States
by Baker & Taylor Publisher Services